Sleeping partner

On Saturday night, as music plays and conversation flows, off-duty DCI David Fyfe is challenged to try and solve an impossible paradox.

An old woman is battered to death and Fyfe is reluctantly tempted to a reunion with a former lover who knows things about him he would much prefer remained a mutual secret.

In a flurry of violence and the short space of forty-eight hours, Fyfe has to piece together the meaning in his encounters with a dying child, a killer Mercedes, a failed suicide attempt, and a new-born baby. When he identifies the murderer his first instinct is to protect him, not arrest him. But it doesn't quite work out that way and Fyfe's sleepless weekend reaches an abrupt and totally unexpected climax.

Sleeping partner is a novel that moves at breakneck pace through a swiftly changing landscape of human emotions where logic and reason are fragile concepts. Fyfe, at the centre of the storm, tries to discover what is right and what is wrong only to find that sometimes they cannot be separated.

SLEEPING PARTNER

William Paul

Constable · London

First published in Great Britain 1996
by Constable & Company Ltd
3 The Lanchesters, 162 Fulham Palace Road
London W6 9ER
Copyright © 1996 by William Paul
The right of William Paul to be
identified as the author of this work
has been asserted by him in accordance
with the Copyright, Designs and Patents Act 1988
ISBN 0 09 475310 5
Set in Linotron Palatino 10 pt by
CentraCet Ltd, Cambridge
Printed in Great Britain by
Hartnolls Ltd, Bodmin

A CIP catalogue record for this book is
available from the British Library

1

Saturday, 23.10

The second surgical glove snapped into the soft flesh above his wrist with a satisfying tightness. The action caused a tiny puff of talcum powder to disperse into the air. There was already a skin of dried superglue painted on each fingertip underneath the thin rubbery surface. Valentine Randolph was nothing if not exceedingly thorough in his preparations.

He held both hands up in front of him and flexed the fingers three times to remove any remaining bubbles of air. He was already wearing a one-piece, dark-coloured overall zipped up to the neck and tucked into socks at the ankles. On his feet he had cheap canvas shoes. On his head he had a closely woven woollen hat pulled down to the top of his ears and his eyebrows. The bulky ridge of wool showed that it would unroll further to cover his whole face. He picked up a pair of dark glasses and put them on to complete the extraordinary outfit. He called it his Saturday Night Special.

He patted the fat bunch of keys in his pocket and checked his watch through the transparent latex sleeve of the glove, having to hold it close to his face to be able to make out the time. It was dark outside, a moonless night with a red sky containing heavy-bellied clouds hanging low and smouldering like a banked-up fire. From his first-floor bedroom window the electronic glow of the hidden city all around him suffused a narrow section of the sky above the tall trees that marked the boundary of his garden. In the distance, bats flickered clumsily across his line of sight. Close up, a large moth tapped its paper-thin wings against the glass, condemned to suicide in hopeless pursuit of a love affair with an unreachable light source.

Randolph turned away from the window and went over to a

table entirely covered by photographs in silver frames. There were pictures of his wedding, of his wife Joan, of himself, and of his family. The three children grew up inside successive frames and then appeared as adults with their own children. He matured from the tall, fresh-faced youth smiling hugely at the church door, to the grandfather with newest grandson on his knee. Joan also grew old in the pictures, transformed from shy, slim bride to proud, Rubenesque matriarch. He reached out and lifted a portrait of her on her own inside a particularly ornate frame. She must have been about forty when it was taken; in her prime, more attractive then than when he first met her. That was more than twenty years ago and, to his loving eye, she had changed little although she had changed such a lot. If there was a life after death, and she had always insisted there was, she would be watching him now, shaking her head at his behaviour, sighing at the confirmation that the loss of her earthly influence had meant him going so badly awry.

He held Joan's picture against his mouth for several seconds, leaving an outline impression of his lips on the damp glass. The oval shape covered her whole face. He wiped it clean with his elbow.

'This one's for you, Joan darling,' he said, as he replaced the frame on the crowded table-top. 'As always.'

A trace of bitter-tasting silver polish had found its way on to his tongue. He tried to spit it out daintily as he made his way downstairs through the empty house with its ghostly furniture and old paintings watching from the walls. In the alcove inside the front door he switched on the alarm at its main console and hurried along the entrance hallway into the kitchen before the time-lapse ran out and the place was filled with a lattice-work of orange laser beams reflecting the particles of drifting dust. At the interior door at the back of the kitchen he programmed another control panel and went down into the garage before another set of lasers kicked in.

The garage was big and spacious, cooler than the house. The air seemed thicker. It smelled of oil and decaying grass cuttings. A long strip light operated by a dangling cord revealed two cars side by side but didn't penetrate to the walls where a host of untidily cluttered shelves and stacks of boxes and garden machinery lurked in the shadows. Randolph moved past the big red Mercedes and slipped into the driver's seat of the white Vauxhall Corsa. He pulled the sun visor down and the ignition keys dropped into his hand. He checked his watch again. Exactly on schedule.

With the engine running quietly, he flicked the remote control that started the door tilting. He couldn't hear the sound of the motor that slowly opened it, showing him the familiar driveway and the grey evening as though somebody was taking a hand away from in front of his eyes. Ahead of him between the two stone gateposts he saw the shape of another small car. He flashed his headlights and the other car returned the message, sending its beams of light off at right angles, pointing the way to be followed and momentarily illuminating in silhouette its lone driver.

Now as Randolph edged his car forward out of the garage the nervousness that he had successfully suppressed while he was getting ready to leave began to affect him. He had to grip the steering wheel tightly to stop his hands trembling. The plastic squeezed them, made them feel uncomfortably dry. He was breathing rapidly, pushing himself back into the driving seat. His stomach felt hollow and his bowels uncomfortably loose. His heartbeat accelerated violently. A sudden stabbing pain in his left shoulder made him wince and reach up to relieve it by pressing hard. The woollen hat made his scalp sweat and when he tried to scratch it his rubber-capped fingers got tangled in his hair and didn't make much difference. He was on the main road and heading into the city at an even pace, well within the speed limit.

Behind him the garage door was folding back into the closed position. It would be simple again tonight, he told himself. Nothing would go wrong. They would come through again and he would have another little trophy to add to his collection in the cupboard.

Randolph had assumed that after a few times he would become hardened and less fearful. But it wasn't turning out like that at all. Each time he went out on the Saturday night trips it seemed to get a little worse. He shifted another notch towards outright terror and panic. The odds against them getting caught were shortening with every outing. He realised that. He had taken that into account at the beginning and he wasn't going to

7

let it stop him no matter how bad it got. That was the best bit of the game anyway. Joan wouldn't have understood but that didn't matter now. He didn't have to explain himself to anyone any more. Wasn't life grand?

2

Saturday, 23.12

Sixty-two, sixty-three. With slow, measured strokes Zena McElhose brushed the mare's tail of silvery grey hair that hung over her shoulder and almost down to her waist. It would be one hundred and twenty strokes for the topside and then the same number for the underside. She had performed the same ritual virtually every night since she was a little girl. Her hair was fine and lustrous. Its whiteness carried with it a certain kind of elegance, the beauty of maturity and experience, symbol of a long life lived wisely and productively. If only now she was able to go back to being a young woman again, to reverse the ageing process that had already taken her beyond her biblical allotted span. If only the silver could be turned back to auburn, and the lines on her face and neck smoothed out, and the dull aching in her ancient bones quietened. If only. If only.

The bedroom seemed to be doubled in size by the number of mirrors. It was one of her self-indulgent vanities: she liked to watch herself when she was alone. She could sit for hours, virtually motionless, trying to catch out the several images by surreptitiously moving a finger that was not part of the reflections. But it was impossible to defeat them as they could so easily defeat her by growing old in front of her eyes. She certainly didn't feel old. Her heart beat powerfully, the blood flowed freely, her mind was undimmed. She was a lonely widow, sitting all alone in her big mansion house with all of her friends dead and her family living far away. She could travel, of course. She was fit enough and could afford it, and she did. But she didn't like to stray too far from home too often, not now. She had intended to take the train down to London to see her grand-daughter Carole. It had been all arranged for the previous night

8

but she had changed her mind at the last moment on the platform with the tickets in her hand. No real reason. Just a whim. She wanted to stay at home. It was her prerogative. She controlled her own life.

The sad widow McElhose, sitting at her dressing-table in her yellow silk robe surrounded by mirrors and perfumes and beauty aids, let the hair fall from her fingers. It fanned cool air against her cheek. Mustn't get morbid, she thought. Mustn't get morose. She had plenty to be thankful for. She was rich and the investment portfolio long-suffering Sidney had bequeathed her was growing nicely. The regular meeting with her lawyer had been a pleasant one on Friday afternoon. If you were the Chancellor the country would be in a far better state, he had joked. Big Gregor always flattered her, always took time to make a fuss of her in his office. She liked it when people took trouble over her. Another of her vanities. It was a harmless failing.

She had her health too, which was more than poor little Lorna in the old lodge by the gates had. A tiny girl, only three years old yet she would almost certainly die soon and there was nothing anybody could do to help her. An expensively dressed old woman with long silver hair wound tightly into a bun would weep at her funeral.

Eight-five, eighty-six. Zena McElhose stood up as she brushed, moving abruptly to clear her head of unwelcome thoughts. The mirror images followed her movements. She would go to church tomorrow morning, she decided. The minister was new. He had a black beard and a burning desire to communicate his belief. She would flirt with him and see if she could manage to give him a red face. He would tolerate her because she made generous donations to the church. She didn't believe there was a God though, never had, never would. Yet nobody suspected her of such heresy. She was an elderly Edinburgh widow, utterly respectable and entirely predictable in all matters. And she would go to church tomorrow and fool them all.

Ninety-seven, ninety-eight. There was a circular turret space adjoining the bedroom. It had tall narrow windows on four sides, a small table and a late Victorian lady's sewing chair in it. With her free hand, Zena lifted the portable phone from its cradle on the bedside table and carried it through the narrow entrance to the turret. She sat in the chair, still brushing, and dialled Carole's number as she looked out into the darkness blanketing her lawns and trees. Sometimes it felt absolutely right to be alone. This was one of those times.

She looked out and saw the sea in the distance. The house had been built by her great, great uncle, a sea captain in the previous century. Beside the bedroom tower was a widow's walk balcony reached by french windows in the first-floor drawing-room. When he was at sea his wife would walk up and down scanning the horizon for his return. He had always come back, according to family legend, eventually dying as an old man after a horse kicked him accidentally during a race meeting on Leith Links.

Zena smiled and lowered her eyes and focused on the much nearer lodge house where little Lorna lay dying. The phone was answered and a faraway voice spoke anxiously in her ear, making her realise at the end of a brush stroke that she had lost count. It must have been one hundred and three, or one hundred and four. She couldn't remember which.

'Granny, is that you?' said Carole. 'I've been trying to phone you all day. Where have you been? Why didn't you come down?'

'Something came up,' Zena lied unashamedly. 'Sorry, but I have to stay here this weekend.'

The brush moved smoothly through her hair. She watched the lights in the house at the end of the drive. One, two . . .

3

Saturday, 23.15
Sandy Ramensky was a huge bear of a man but surprisingly light on his feet. The army had taught him to be a boxer and he had won the inter-regimental title. He hadn't kept up the boxing when he finished his time. It came too easily to him. He enjoyed it too much and it conflicted with his natural disinclination to hurt people. He didn't like violence. He couldn't stand pain. As a child he was always being accused of being too soft. Big certainly, but soft.

Ramensky walked with a purposeful stride. His arms moved back and forward, the hands balled into big fists. He walked with his head down, his coat flowing behind him like the cloak of a pantomime villain. The pavements were busy with Saturday night drinkers and party-goers but he carved a path through them, never looking up or to the side. He turned into the park, on to the walkway lined by avenues of trees. Globe-topped white lights hung among the branches like a daisy chain of miniature moons, scattering confetti shadows as leaves and branches tossed and twisted in the wind. Wrapped in his own private world, he was unaware of the noise of the other people on the streets fading into the distance behind him. The park after dark was a taboo place to most people on their own, its interweaved paths and swathes of grass the haunt of professional muggers and roaming gangs of youths. Ramensky didn't think about it. He didn't care.

It was the unfairness that bothered Ramensky; the inescapable inequity in what was happening to him and Marianne. There was no reason, no explanation, no discernible purpose behind it. Pent-up frustration fuelled his movements, making every step he took an angry stamp on the unyielding ground. His jaw was sore because he kept grinding his teeth. He gripped pools of sweat, like precious possessions, in his tightly clenched hands.

That evening, as he did almost every evening, he had sat in his claustrophobic security booth in the basement of the high-rise office block and tried to find some sense in the horror that had invaded his life. He must have missed something, some miserable fact, some evasive clue that might explain why. There must be something, some cause to the effect. Was he stupid? Why couldn't he see it?

And all evening he watched the six grey squares of the closed-circuit television screens as they lazily flipped between the underground garage and the internal corridors leading towards his booth. Occasionally people appeared like underwater creatures scuttling for shelter. They flashed identity cards he looked right through and didn't see. And every second hour he left the screens and did his rounds, slamming the key into the special terminals on the different floors, trying to rip the apparatus from the wall. It was a simple routine, giving him plenty of time to think before his shift ended and he handed over to Eddie with mutual monosyllabic grunts. All night the thoughts swirled inside his brain, never giving him a moment's peace. One obsessive question demanded an answer he could not find. Why? Why his beautiful little daughter? Why his only child? Why was Lorna dying?

Ramensky stopped instinctively. There were four of them, two directly in front of him, two sliding sideways to get round him. He raised his head slowly, assimilating the situation in a single glance, feeling the rapid build-up of an adrenalin rush. He took a step backwards to keep the two fringers in view and balanced himself on the balls of his feet. His hands came up to waist level, fists relaxing. All tension left his body. He was able to forget everything but his immediate surroundings. A half-smile tickled the edges of his mouth.

'Okay, big boy. Let's see what you've got.'

Ramensky's mind snapped into narrow focus. Everything else was shut out apart from the semicircle of fragile bodies converging on him. It had happened when he won the army boxing championship; total and absolute concentration. He seemed to be able to move at twice the speed of his lumbering opponent, his bloodied glove hammering again and again into the helpless face as his victim hung on the ropes. The referee couldn't drag Ramensky off alone. It took his own seconds to jump into the ring and join in. He won but, once he had calmed down, the manner of his victory scared him.

Now it was happening again. A gust of wind set the trees in motion and the world slowed down around him. But this time his purpose wasn't a garish silver trophy and the adulation of his friends. This time it was the chance to save Lorna. Here was his way out of frustration. Here was his purpose. Now he understood. He would kill these bad people. He would tear off their heads and steal the life-force within them. And then his dear, beautiful, innocent Lorna would be saved. Here was the explanation he had been seeking. Here was his reason. It all suddenly made sense. This was Lorna's chance, maybe her only chance.

Ramensky saw the shape to his right crouch and lunge. He swung his arm and caught the onrushing attacker on the side of the head. It was more a slap than a punch; his hand covered the face from chin to crown, felt rough stubble on the jaw, the bony shape of an eye socket, the hair-line of the scalp. Ramensky lifted him off the ground and flung him full length, arms and legs

12

spread wide. He rode a wave of moving shadows to land shoulder first on the ground ten feet away and began to scramble to his feet. Ramensky made a grab at the shape to his left but it was already gone, stepping through the row of trees and lamp-posts and into the darkness beyond. Ramensky turned back to the front but the other two were also running, disappearing. Only the one he had hit remained, falling as he tried to get up, whimpering with terror as he finally managed to stay upright. Ramensky grabbed the collar of his jacket but he wriggled free of it. Ramensky roared like an animal and chased him along the white-lit pathway. The boy gave one frantic, wild-eyed look back and dodged to the side, instantly swallowed by the darkness.

Ramensky stopped. The moment had passed. He had failed to seize it. It vanished into the darkness. Lorna would die. Nothing made sense any more. A huge sadness overwhelmed him, making him feel cold as if he had stepped into a body of deep water. He looked round in bewilderment. The wind blew against his face like a blast of some monster's fetid breath. Ramensky's whole body seemed to contract and shrink. The tightness of his clenched fists was painful. He lowered his head and stared at the ground. He took one faltering step, then another, then another. Gradually he found a rhythm to the movement. It allowed him not to think.

4

Saturday, 23.21
Hilary's frothy mane of light brown curls framed a smiling face that looked up at David Fyfe with openly immodest curiosity. She was small and intensely sexy, with a jumble of gold chains in the hollow of her throat above a tight black dress that ended well above the knees and enhanced the rounded curves of breasts and hips. She was sitting straight-backed, her legs crossed at the ankle. The hemline rode high as she leaned forward from the waist and gently tapped the wineglass he had just handed her against the glass he held in his own hand. They teased each other with party-goers' idle banter.

'You're taking very good care of me,' she said.

'My pleasure, I assure you,' he replied. 'If there's anything else I can do for you just let me know.'

'As a matter of fact there is something you can do.'

'What's that?'

'Talk to me.'

'Is that all?'

'For the moment.'

Her smile widened to show even teeth. She ran her tongue ostentatiously over her lower lip and sat back. The gold chains rolled and shone. The black dress adjusted itself round her like a second skin, moving fractionally up her thigh. Fyfe lowered himself into the space beside her on the two-seater sofa. She half turned, putting one leg over the other and a hand palm-down on her knee. Fyfe glanced across the other side of the room but couldn't see Sally. He looked back into Hilary's pale blue eyes, smiled and tried to relax.

'Go on then,' she said. 'Talk to me.'

So he began talking, eyes drawn to the perfect blackness of Hilary's dress where it was surrounded by the creamy whiteness of arms and throat, her darkly shining legs and the slender fingers which waved expressively in the air. He could feel himself already falling into the centre of that unknown but welcoming total blackness. Hilary was lovely and dangerous. Sexual tension crackled across the air between them. His instincts were raw-edged and receptive. He blinked slowly and she didn't go away. He resigned himself to his fate.

Fyfe hadn't wanted to go to the party. It was an Edinburgh New Town affair, full of Sally's university friends and colleagues. He wouldn't fit in. He had nothing in common with any of them. He wouldn't know anybody. Sally insisted, wheedling at first, then disappointed, then threatening. He had complained continuously, but eventually he gave in and the upshot was they arrived late at the party. There was much kissing of cheeks, and shaking of hands, and introductions promptly forgotten. Sally guided him into the centre of the party crowd and drifted away on the social round. He swallowed his first glass of wine in a single gulp and decided he would just have to get drunk and bear it.

That was when he saw Hilary in her little black dress.

14

Suddenly he was glad he had been persuaded to come after all. She caught him looking her up and down and their silent exchange of knowing smiles sparked an instant mutual attraction. She was standing on her own under a central archway which divided the large room into two sections. Unbroken eye contact established a momentary intimacy that excluded every other person present. He told her his name and she told him hers. They discovered both were partners who grudged being dragged along. Forming a natural alliance they moved away from the crowd through the arch to the quieter side of the room and the unoccupied sofa by one of the windows. A tall standard lamp cast subdued lighting in the corner. Fyfe collected drinks and settled down beside his new-found friend, knowing already that he was going to regret this night ending too soon.

They chatted amiably, not giving much away except superficial information about families and everyday life. Fyfe didn't mention how his fondness for attractive women like her caused him problems in the past. He pointed out his wife Sally but didn't explain the awkward bit about them being divorced and reconciled without actually remarrying. Hilary pointed out her husband Brian, as tall as the standard lamp, and Fyfe wondered what she wasn't telling about him and their marriage. She was a computer operator, keener on sport than work. Not a career woman, but somebody who liked to live well so she was obliged to work. If she had the money to begin with, she wouldn't bother to work. It was a meeting of minds.

Fyfe resented it when Brian came over to interrupt their brief conversation. They shook hands, exchanged pleasantries, and then Hilary was led away to be introduced to someone else. She glanced back wistfully over her shoulder as she went. He appreciated the rear view of her and thought maybe she was putting a little extra swing into her walk just for his benefit.

The party went on around him. It seemed to get more crowded. The music seemed to get louder. He helped himself to some food from the spread in the kitchen and got drawn into a group of strangers. He was relaxed, drinking steadily and beginning to enjoy himself. He annoyed a fat woman in a Paisley pattern kaftan by refusing to agree that most police forces were riddled with corruption. And once he had made a plea for a quick return to the death penalty offered to have any of her outstanding

15

parking fines cancelled for a small fee. She didn't have much of a sense of humour, but she laughed when his half quail egg fell off his bit of toasted bread and was tramped into the carpet.

He joined Sally and she introduced him to some more people. He managed to manoeuvre himself into a position beside Hilary but Brian was beside her with a proprietary arm linked to hers as he discussed internal university politics with an old man who stood out because he was wearing a dinner suit among all the open-necked shirts and jeans. 'Dean of the faculty,' Sally explained quietly. 'Likes to keep certain standards.'

They circulated. A skinny guy with incongruously fat hands and a tweed jacket trapped Fyfe beside the bookcase. He was a philosopher, he said, working on a radical new theory to explain Zeno's paradox. He was drunk. He kept touching Fyfe on the elbow as he invited him to create a mind picture of Achilles and a tortoise. Fyfe wasn't really listening, but his frown must have made it seem as if he was concentrating hard on the mental problem. In fact he was trying as politely as he could to watch Hilary over the hound's tooth check landscape of the philosopher's shoulder.

'All motion and change are illusions,' the philosopher said. 'I'll show you. Think of the distance between this side of the room and that side.'

Fyfe estimated the distance between him and Hilary as maybe twenty feet. She was standing side on to him, slipping scraps of toast covered with quail's eggs and red caviare into her mouth.

'Now, to reach the other side you first have to travel half the distance. Am I correct?'

Fyfe thought about it and nodded, knowing there must be a catch.

'And before you reach the half-way point you first have to travel half of the distance towards it.'

'That's right,' Fyfe agreed.

'And to get to that point you have to travel half-way towards it.'

'So?'

'There's always another half-way.'

'Is there?'

'Don't you see?' the philosopher said earnestly. 'Logically you

16

can keep splitting the distance in half an infinite number of times.'

'So?'

'So, it means you never reach the other side of the room.'

'But I can.' He looked over at Hilary and saw the rippling movement of her cheekbones under her skin as her teeth bit down on a piece of toast. 'I can walk over right now and touch it if I want to.'

'That's the point.'

'Is it?'

'That's why it's a paradox. You can do it but the point is that you shouldn't be able to.'

Fyfe thought about it and rapidly reached a philosophical dead end. It was true as far as he could see, but it was also untrue. A real paradox he could annoy the boys with next time there was a session in the pub. The philosopher grinned, banana-mouthed, and started to haver on about Immanuel Kant. At one stage he realised that Fyfe wasn't paying attention and followed his line of sight to where Hilary was standing by the fireplace throwing the occasional bored glance in his direction.

'Aha,' said the philosopher, tapping the side of his nose. 'Sometimes a boisterous passion hurries our thoughts, as a hurricane does our bodies, without leaving us the liberty of thinking on other things.'

'I'm sorry?' Fyfe said.

'Locke. His essay concerning human understanding.'

'Really?'

'And did anybody?'

'Did anybody what?'

'Understand his essay?'

Hilary crossed the distance between them without apparent hold-up or difficulty and rescued Fyfe. She murmured an apology to the drunken philosopher and pulled Fyfe to one side so they could speak alone.

'I have to go now.'

'Do you really? It's early yet.' Fyfe looked at his watch. It was well after midnight. He hadn't noticed the time passing.

'Give me your arm,' she said.

He did as he was told. She pushed the sleeve of his shirt up to

17

the elbow and turned it to the smooth, relatively hairless underside. She held his wrist and wrote a number. The sharp tip of the pen pressed deeply into the soft skin. Its touch was cold, like teeth playfully nibbling. Hilary signed her name below the number with a flourish. Fyfe tilted his head to one side to be able to read it.

'Just so you won't forget me,' she said, holding on to his wrist longer than was necessary.

'I wouldn't do that.'

'Call me.'

'I will.'

'Promise.'

'I promise.'

She left him, heading for the door where her husband Brian appeared to drape a coat over her shoulders among a crowd of other departing couples. Sally was suddenly beside Fyfe. He rolled down his sleeve. More secrets to keep, he thought.

'Ready to go?' Sally asked.

'Yes,' he replied.

'You seemed to enjoy yourself. It wasn't so bad, was it? After all your complaining too.'

'No,' he admitted. 'It wasn't so bad.'

He kissed Sally's cheek guiltily, knowing from experience that she would want to make love when they got home. Hilary had slipped from Fyfe's sight but not his mind. In it he was able to follow her out and watch her gradually blend with the darkness, joining the other creatures of the night who inhabited the city and over whom he had no control. There were other things moving out there in the darkness too, so many different things, things that would affect him whether he liked it or not. The flesh of his arms prickled coldly where Hilary had written her name.

'Shall we?' Sally said, tugging at his arm. 'Come on, let's go. Stop dreaming. You were a million miles away there.'

Not far enough, Fyfe thought.

5

Sunday, 00.27

Zena McElhose had her eyes open behind the mask. A cluster of pink-tinged white lights appeared like splashes of paint thrown against a wall and faded quickly. Then another one, then another one, in a silent, almost colourless fireworks display. She tried to impose some pattern of shape and coherence on the shifting lights but as soon as she identified one it was already dissolving and she could not be sure she had seen it in the first place. Eventually she grew tired of the game and pushed her sleep mask up on to her forehead.

It was impossible for her to sleep. Her mind was racing, flicking over dozens of trivial things she had done, or hadn't done, or was planning to do. There was a new garden hose to buy, her magazine subscriptions to renew, competitions she wanted to enter, letters to be written, and it was her turn to choose the flowers for the church next week.

She did have a supply of sleeping pills but preferred not to take them. She regretted having had a nap in the middle of the afternoon, but she had fallen asleep listening to a boring radio play. It had been about a widow who placed an advertisement in the lonely hearts column of her local newspaper and then didn't have the courage to actually meet any of the men who replied. Or at least she hadn't by the time Zena nodded off. Maybe she did find true love in the end and lived happily ever after. Zena would never know. When she woke with a start the radio had moved on to a programme about the potential for recycling plastic bottles.

She climbed out of bed and the surrounding images converged inwards on her from the mirrors. She stepped into her slippers and tied her robe loosely around her. She picked up her wedding ring from the dressing-table and put it on her finger where it fitted snugly into the groove worn in her skin. Sidney watched her from the crowd of family pictures. She caught a glimpse of another fainter image in the thin glass over the photographs.

She went downstairs to the kitchen and opened a vacuum-packed bag of fresh coffee. The rich aroma spilled from the bag with an almost physical presence as she poured it into the filter. The machine gurgled and burped and leaked its end product into the glass container. Zena stood beside it with her face right up close, holding her hair back out of the way, watching intently. She wasn't really interested in drinking the coffee but she liked to smell it and watch it being made.

She didn't hear so much as sense the movement behind her. She was just idly wondering how she would fill her day and had remembered she intended going to church, when she turned round. It was a reflex action, done without thinking. The casual surprise of seeing someone beside her in the kitchen congealed immediately into shock and her whole body trembled with a terrible upwelling of fear that was just as quickly suppressed. What was happening, she wondered rationally? Maybe she had had a black-out? Her sense of time was displaced. She ran the events of the day over in her mind and still got all the way to her own kitchen where she stood now. Fear returned. Something was wrong.

'What are you doing here?' Zena asked.

There was no reply from the familiar face, just a blank stare and a sudden convulsion that seemed to affect the whole room. There was a shout from far away and an explosion of pink-tinged white light blocked out everything else. Zena found herself on the floor, her cheek pressed against the coldness of the vinyl covering. She expected the light to fade as it always did behind the mask but instead it grew brighter, and pinker, changing to red, a deep scarlet blood red. And the cold of her cheek started burning and she couldn't understand why she didn't feel the pain when it came roaring up through her fragile body, exploding it apart and killing her dead.

6

Sunday, 08.25
Marianne Dunne opened the bedroom door and looked in on her daughter. The grinning Disney characters cavorted silently around the walls and spilled down on to the duvet on the bed. Lorna was lying on her stomach, face turned away towards the window where the dawn light was beginning to lighten the air behind the drawn curtains. Fine strands of blonde hair did not make a thick enough covering to hide the crown of her head. An arm lying on the pillow had the plastic apparatus for easy delivery of drugs taped to it, its tapering blue permanently inserted into a vein. All round it the skin was light blue, tending to green like a spillage of oil on a desert of white sand.

Marianne watched, checking for the slight rise and fall of the girl's shoulders that showed she was breathing. She couldn't see anything moving. A flutter of alarm made her take three quick steps across the room just as she convinced herself she was wrong, that there was movement. Her head touched the cardboard mobile hanging from the light fitting. The carousel of colourful ponies and clowns flapped round in an unsteady circle swinging against each other.

It was here she had found Sandy standing last night staring down on Lorna. The carousel had been in silent motion then. He always set it going when he came into the bedroom. It was the first thing he did, a flick of the wrist and off it went, spinning and gradually slowing until it came to a complete standstill. It was like Lorna's life, he had once told her in a tone of voice that made her skin crawl; you can't see what's stopping it but you know that very soon it is going to come to an end.

Marianne reached out and held her hand a few inches from Lorna's sleeping head. Goofy and Donald Duck lay hideously deformed among the creases of the duvet bundle. Behind her the carousel slowed and stopped. She backed away, satisfied her daughter was still alive. For the time being at least.

Outside a steady drizzle leaked from a leaden sky. Marianne

pulled her front door shut behind her and hurried up the broad driveway to the big house, holding her coat tightly at her throat without bothering to fasten it. She shuffled awkwardly along, scraping her well-worn slippers against the ground to prevent herself stepping out of them. A huge black and white seagull stood on the lawn. Another was perched on the railing of the widow's walk on the first floor. There were other gulls on the rooftops of the houses beyond the trees. Birds flying low inshore always presaged stormy weather.

Marianne was late. Mrs McElhose hated it if her early morning coffee wasn't ready on time. She broke into a shambling trot as she crossed the expanse of gravel at the front of the house. She went right past the front door and down the narrow path at the side of the patio at the rear. She bent down to pick up the small statue of a frog beside the rusty boot cleaner and retrieved the back door key from its hiding place. She was surprised to find the door unlocked. But it was still stiff, requiring a good shove to open it and another to close it behind her.

She was in the outer kitchen with its flagstone floor and ancient head-high fireplace now blocked off and converted into a wall of shelves full of little-used garden equipment and other junk. Marianne took off her coat as she went to the inner door, an incongruously modern stainless steel design with frosted glass that led into the kitchen proper. The coat was draped over her arm as she pushed the door open and mounted the six-inch step. The strong aroma of coffee confused her. There shouldn't be such a smell. She hadn't made any coffee yet. Mrs McElhose never made her own in the mornings. Maybe her granddaughter Carole had arrived unexpectedly as she sometimes did. That was a possibility. Yet there were no cars in the drive. She might have flown north, taken a taxi in from the airport. But then surely she would have heard it coming past the gates.

Marianne stood in the middle of the kitchen and looked down on Mrs McElhose's body on the floor at her feet. Her long silver grey hair had been stained pink by the blood that spread out in a halo round her head. The skin of her face was a livid white, cracked and scored like the surface of a crocodile skin bag. The red bruise was like a carnation, like the one Marianne had worn on her handbag at her cousin's wedding and kept in a glass of water on the windowsill for a week afterwards. She stared,

22

automatically checking for signs of breathing and seeing none. She reached out and held her hand a few inches from Mrs McElhose's head, sensing only the coldness of death.

It was then she screamed. A deep-seated, penetrating shriek of protest and fear that hurt her throat. She turned and ran, still screaming as she stumbled over the flagstones and took several attempts to wrench open the back door. She ran up the path at the side of the house, leaving her slippers in her wake. She didn't feel the rough gravel under the soles of her feet. The seagull on the lawn spread its wings and lifted clumsily into the air. The one on the railing of the widow's walk swooped down and only just seemed to avoid colliding with the ground before it started to gain height again. On the tarmac driveway Marianne ran blindly into the arms of Sandy. The sight of him shocked her into silence. He was wearing only a thin T-shirt and jeans. His feet, like hers, were bare.

'What is it?' he shouted, holding her at arm's length and gripping her shoulders so tightly it hurt. 'I heard you scream.'

She struggled to find the words to explain and be able to breathe at the same time. She pointed back at the house. Saliva blocked the back of her mouth and caused her to cough. The shadow of a gull passed over them, darkening their faces.

'She's dead,' she managed to say finally. 'In the kitchen. She's been killed.'

'Call the police.'

Sandy left her where she stood and ran towards the house, disappearing down the same side path she had just come up. She looked from the big house down to her own house at the entrance gates. Lorna would be on her own, she realised with a heart-tugging pull of anxiety. Lorna might wake up and not know where anyone was. Lorna might panic. She might die all alone. Marianne, limping as belated pain asserted itself in her bruised feet, hurried home to make sure it didn't happen.

Sunday, 08.47

On the freshly mown first tee at the Monarch's Course at Gleneagles Sir Duncan Morrison, Chief Constable and six handicap golfer, addressed the ball. The horseshoe of people around him settled into impatient quietness as they waited for the first blow of the annual Edinburgh versus Glasgow senior police officers' challenge to be struck. Early rain had passed over and the sun had come out. The smell of cut grass was in the air. Tea and bacon rolls had been served in the hotel, gossip exchanged, and raffle tickets sold. Now the serious business was about to begin. Bracken Brae, three hundred and ninety-four yards to the south-east, was the first hole. Beyond it was the glen of the eagles, the undulating Perthshire countryside and, on the horizon, the cloud-shrouded Ochil Hills where the rain had gone.

Sir Duncan had on all the gear. A Titleist visor, Pringle jumper, plus-twos, tartan socks, and black and white brogues. He waggled his driver, waggled his hips, and chewed on the stem of his pipe. It travelled from one corner of his mouth to the other as he raised the club back to shoulder height with practised slowness. The dimpled white ball was all shiny and wet on its bright red wooden tee.

Go on, David Fyfe thought maliciously. Dig a big divot out and make an arse of yourself.

The club swung down and hit the ball on the sweet spot. It cracked away along the fairway, perfectly straight except for a slight fade at the end of its flight which meant it landed and bounced towards the green perfectly. Sir Duncan stood in freeze farme, his arms wrapped round his neck, a triumphant puff of smoke emerging from the bowl of his pipe. The spectators applauded appreciatively. Fyfe grudgingly joined in as the rival Chief Constable, William Marshall, bent down to tee up his ball. He was the product of another collision with the expensive clothes section in the professionals' shop and another low handicapper. His red leather golf bag had as many strategic bulges as a drug-pumped weightlifter. His ball followed the exact line of Sir Duncan's, dropping just short of its length into the hollow in front of the slightly elevated green. There was more generous applause.

'Let that be a lesson to you,' Marshall said out loud. 'Keep your bad shots for the parts of the course where you don't have an audience.'

Everybody laughed. The two chiefs climbed into their motorised golf buggy and hummed away on the concrete track along the side of the fairway. The next pair occupied the tee.

Fyfe and his opponent, Detective Inspector Eric Bradley, knew each other fairly well from joint operations on the crime squad. They had played together before too and Fyfe had never beaten him. They were eighth of the twelve pairs to go so had plenty of time to spare. They strolled over to the putting green behind the starter's hut and began to knock a few balls about. Fyfe was worried about making a fool of himself. Not only were his eyes sticky with lack of sleep after his late night but he hadn't been playing regularly at all, hadn't had a game for at least six months. When he had dug his clubs out of the cupboard under the stairs he found a mouldy growth on the heads of the woods and rust specks on the irons.

'Have a late night, did you, Davie?' Bradley asked.

'Does it show?'

'No more than usual for you, but you seem quieter. Something bothering you? Been working too hard?'

'I'll liven up. I just need a few birdies to put me in the mood.'

He aimed for a hole about five yards from him marked by a small metal flag. The ball missed by six inches on the left and travelled at least ten feet past. He tried again with another ball. It traced a path through the rain-soaked grass and stopped well short.

'So how's things with you anyway?' Bradley said.

'Same as ever,' Fyfe replied, head down over a ball as he tried another putt. 'Nothing new.'

There was something new though. Hilary was new. He couldn't stop thinking about her, all gift-wrapped in her little black dress and her sensually pleading eyes. He checked his forearm for the phone number she had written there. He'd had a quick shower that morning before setting off, protecting his arm from the water so that it wouldn't be washed clean. He didn't know if it was her home or her office number. He didn't know how she would respond if he phoned her anyway. Without the party atmosphere, the drink and the illusion of intimacy, maybe she would be acutely embarrassed to hear from him. He had had enough trouble with women in the past. Maybe it would be for the best if he left Hilary well alone. He tried a short, straight putt. It hit the flag and bounced off at a sharp angle.

'Are we going to make this interesting, or what?' Bradley asked.

'It's for the greater glory of the force. Can it be more interesting than that?'

'Oh, I think so. How about a pound a hole and a fiver on the match?'

'And nips for birdies?'

'Of course,' Bradley said.

'And you give me six strokes.'

'Yes. Six and the pleasure of my company.'

'You're on.'

Fyfe moved even closer to a hole and managed to sink his first putt of the day. He was thinking that he would only phone Hilary if he won this match against Bradley. That would save him from having to make a decision one way or the other; it would be made for him. If he won he would call her up. If he lost he would take another shower and wash her away. That was settled.

Fyfe lined up a long putt. He hit the ball far too hard. It scooted across the wet grass and would have gone racing past but it clanked into the metal flag, jumped two feet in the air and vanished into the hole.

'That's more like it,' Fyfe said, grinning over at Bradley. 'Now I'm getting the hang of this game.'

8

Detective Inspector John Sapalski examined the old woman's body, curiously curled like an acrobat in mid-flight, and the rubber-thick blood on the kitchen floor beside her. The dent in the side of her skull had a distinctive lattice pattern on the damaged flesh. The rich smell of the over-brewed coffee seemed to pour down from the worktop and cover the body like a transparent fog. Sapalski felt the nausea rise in his gorge and squeeze into the back of his mouth. He swallowed, grimacing at the vileness of the taste. He stayed where he was, squatting down, letting a wave of dizziness pass, hoping that no one behind him would notice how badly it was affecting him.

He might be young and raw but he had dealt with dead bodies before, car accident victims mostly when he was on the roads, still warm and bleeding in their twisted metal coffins. There had been a fair number of stabbings too once he had become a detective, and a strangling, and a shotgun killing that had blasted through a skull as if it was a ripe orange. Man's inhumanity to man was rarely pretty though he could remember one call-out when they had found a young woman's body provocatively draped over the top of a bed, all made-up and dressed in an elegant silk nightdress. There were four of them and they stood looking down on her for much longer than necessary. She was absolutely lovely and they were all wondering what had happened in her life to make death seem so attractive to her that she could so apparently calmly take an overdose and induce heart failure. Something had driven her over the edge and it must have been bad, very bad. But they never had found out the real reason.

Sapalski looked down on the pathetic dead body of Zena McElhose. This was different. This was not suicide. It was a killing and any idea that it might have been an accident caused by her falling and striking her head on a sharp corner somewhere was easily dismissed. Evidence for that would have been immediately obvious but the kitchen was immaculately clean and ordered with not a pot or pan out of place. The violence was contained closely around the huddled body on the floor and he was in charge of finding out what had happened, the first time he had had to call the shots in a murder investigation as opposed to simply following orders. A few years from now he would look back on it as a character-building experience. In the meantime, with the shock of death and the weight of responsibility, he would be doing well to keep the contents of his hurried breakfast down.

Sapalski stood up slowly and turned to face the two uniforms who were with him in the kitchen and the big bruiser of an odd job man who had found the body. Forensic were on their way. The crime scene was sealed. He reached out and flicked off the gurgling coffee machine with a fingernail. He hadn't forgotten anything.

The big man had been standing at the front of the house when Sapalski had arrived simultaneously with the uniforms in a dramatic hee-hawing of sirens and spray of gravel. In his bare feet, he had taken them down a side path and in the back door to show them the mortal remains of poor Mrs McElhose. Now he stood uneasily in front of Sapalski, refusing to look at him directly, opening and closing his huge fists. Sapalski tried to find some fellow feeling for their shared Polish heritage but there was no empathy there, no acknowledgement, no easy banter about where their parents and grandparents hailed from. He didn't want to be prejudiced against the big man but it was hard. There was an emptiness in his eyes. He looked dangerous. He had to be a suspect.

'You found her as she is lying now, Mr Ramensky?'

'No. Marianne found her.'

'Ah yes. Your wife found her. It is your wife, isn't it?'

'Yes. Common law wife.'

'And she keeps her own name.'

'We like it that way.'

Marianne Dunne was being questioned by Detective Sergeant Graham Blair. She was too distressed to return to the big house, she said. Sapalski couldn't handle weeping women. He was glad to delegate the job to Blair. Let her pull herself together a bit before he had to face her.

'She comes up every morning to make Mrs McElhose's breakfast,' Ramensky was explaining. 'The key is under the frog at the door. I heard her scream. I came running up. This is what I saw.'

'What exactly is your role in the household?'

'I do the gardens, a bit of painting. Sometimes I would drive her to the shops.' He shrugged. 'I work elsewhere as a security guard.'

'And your wife was the housekeeper?'

'Something like that. She only did breakfast.'

'Not evening meals.'

'Never in the evening.'

'Why not?'

'She had to stay in. I work in the evenings mostly. Besides, Mrs McElhose liked to be on her own without fuss.'

'You said your wife had to stay in. Why?'

'Our daughter Lorna.'

'How old is Lorna?'

'Three.'

'No grandparents? No babysitters? Couldn't she come up here as well?'

'No. Lorna is ill and can never be left alone. One of us always has to be with her.'

'What's wrong with her?'

Ramensky lifted his head and stared straight at Sapalski. His mouth flickered in a sneer then his body settled into a posture of weary resignation with his fists loosely clenched by his sides. Sapalski wished he hadn't asked the question. He was due to be a father soon. His wife was heavily pregnant. He constantly dreamed about healthy babies and rosy-cheeked young children bouncing on his knee. He regarded his wife's swollen stomach containing the promise of new life with awe and reverence. Now he was going to hear about an alternative version of fatherhood and it was going to be horrible.

'Because she could die at any moment. She has leukaemia.'

The nausea forced its way back up Sapalski's throat. He coughed and a liquid squirted against the inside of his mouth. He had to swallow it again, trying not to make too much of a show of how distasteful it was. Now it was his turn to avoid eye contact, regretting his aggressive line of questioning. He rubbed his dry lips and half turned to face a door he hadn't noticed before. He needed to change the subject.

'Have you checked the rest of the house?' he asked.

'I haven't gone beyond the kitchen,' Ramensky said. 'I never thought. It's only been an hour since we called.'

The uniforms shook their heads to confirm they hadn't looked further either. There was a knock on the outer door and the doctor arrived with the first of the forensic team. An unwieldy stainless steel box was lugged over beside the dead body and the doctor began surveying it with detached professional curiosity. Sapalski went over to the other door. Ramensky followed him, moving disconcertingly lightly for such a big man.

'Where does it lead?' Sapalski asked.

'It comes out behind the main staircase at the entrance hall.'

Sapalski went through slowly, feeling vaguely absurd but unwilling to rush it just in case there really was a psychotic murderer lying in wait for his next victim. The hall was empty. Its arched ceiling was reflected dully in the polished marble floor tiles. Carved wooden doorways, antique tables and coat stands lined the walls. There was a hollow elephant's foot full of umbrellas and walking-sticks. A life-size porcelain Dalmatian watched him with a haughty expression. A huge mirror in an ornate gilt frame made the dog one of a pair and doubled the size of the place. Beside Sapalski the stairs rose to the first floor, slightly tarnished brass carpet rods slotted across each step. At the other end of the hall a door with stained glass in its top half was ajar, giving on to a large alcove with the main outside door behind it. Ramensky grunted and pointed to the alcove. Sapalski followed the line of his finger and saw what was holding the inner door open. It was the sole of a shoe, attached to an ankle.

Sapalski ran forward. He did not hear Ramensky beside him but knew he was there. The door opened freely to reveal a body face down on the floor, one arm outstretched ahead of it, fingers curled round a large-headed mallet used for tenderising meat. The first thought into Sapalski's head was that it was like the Statue of Liberty in overalls, the second that it was like a swimmer doing the front crawl. His third thought was more of a question. Why did the body have a head knitted out of wool? The answer, he realised, was that it was wearing a terrorist-style balaclava.

30

Sapalski knelt down, noticing more and more details. The overalls were cheap and shiny. The outstretched hand looked waxen and barely human. The fingers did not seem to be quite grasping the mallet properly. There was blood on the jagged surface of the mallet head. He had found murderer and murder weapon in another clearly defined pool of latent violence, contained by unaffected ordinary surroundings like the victim back in the kitchen. But there was no obvious wound on this man. What had killed him?

'He's not dead,' Ramensky said.

'What?'

'Look. He's still breathing.'

Sapalski pulled the overall collar down and the balaclava up to the chin, searching for a pulse on the side of the neck. He found it, a very faint beat of blood but enough to show he was indeed still alive. Sapalski rolled the man on to his back, stripped the balaclava from his face and began to give him the kiss of life.

'Get an ambulance,' he shouted between breaths, sensing that Ramensky was still standing over him.

And as Sapalski blew more air through the cold lips of the motionless body he saw a bloated bluish-green bruise on its pale forehead and a trickle of blood that seemed to come from the corner of an eye, like a tear. And as he lowered his lips on to the cold flesh of the unconscious man he was able to make out the outline in sweat of a bare footprint on the tiles just in front of the impassive Dalmatian's paws. Within the space of three deep breaths and exhalations the footprint had evaporated and vanished.

9

Sunday, 10.20

The hymn-singing was slow and frustrating, ponderous voices struggling to maintain a decent pace through the verses. Maureen Gilliland stood alone in her family pew with the hymn book laid flat in the palm of her right hand and moved her lips without uttering a sound to compete with the wheezing of the organ, the creaking of the upright wooden-walled pews, and the

31

rhythmic moaning of the congregation. The hymn book wasn't open at the right page anyway.

Looking out over the top of her half-moon glasses she saw the minister as a roly-poly black and white smudge above the shifting landscape of hats and balding heads. Her short-sightedness caused the back-lit cross hanging above the pulpit to lose its branching arms and become a single shaft of fuzzy light like the flame trail of a rocket taking off. The pair of stained glass windows behind were patchworks of multi-coloured sunshine. The arched ceiling flowing from the line of tall stone pillars was a grey blur of solidity, as though somebody had stuffed the roof space with cotton wool.

Maureen's thoughts were wholly unsynchronised with her outward appearance of a middle-aged woman in her Sunday best dress at morning service. All she could think of as the people around her in the church praised the Lord was how she desperately wanted to break one of the ten commandments: Thou shalt not commit adultery. She wanted to and she wanted to do it with her long-time boss, Valentine Randolph. She had come to church that morning all puffed up with courage to lean forward to the row in front where he always sat, tap him on the shoulder and whisper secretly that she was ready now. Of course, it wasn't just to be one of those fleeting secretary-boss things. They had been together too long for that. More than twenty years, and she pretended to herself she had enough Christian respect to suppress her desires and wait for a proper interval after the death of his wife. Technically, it would not be adultery, of course, because he was a widower and she was unmarried. But it would feel like adultery because the desire had been with her for so long. He was free now, and so was she; free to declare her love and surrender herself to him.

Except he wasn't there. She had never known him not to be there on a Sunday morning when he had nothing else planned. It was totally out of character. Unless there was a good reason he always attended church, and she knew there wasn't one because she presided over his diary, both social and business. This weekend had been a normal one. He hadn't been booked to go anywhere.

Maureen, vicious butterflies thrashing about in her stomach, had anticipated returning to his house and letting him make love to her there. He might have been shocked at her forwardness, but no doubt delighted. He had propositioned her after all, blatantly tearing down the formal barrier that had separated them as employer and employee. He had made the first move. She had hesitated but now she was keen to seal the bond between them with a rush of physical energy.

She had never married, never even slept with a man in her forty-two years. Valentine knew that. He had told her he knew that and it made her doubly exciting for him. She had thought sex was something she would never experience and it had not seemed that great a sacrifice, but just lately it had been nagging at her again, distracting her. Dormant hormones were stirring unaccountably, and then there was Valentine, the man whom she now realised she regarded as a husband in every sense but the biological one. He had changed radically since his wife's death, become more extrovert, more demonstrative, more access- ible. He touched her when previously he scrupulously avoided contact. He kissed her. He made suggestions. Sometimes he worried her. He told her what he wanted to do to her and she trembled with the force of the wicked desire it kindled inside her.

Why should she not go for it? Time was short and she craved excitement. She had taken stock of a blameless life and was ready to embrace sin eagerly, unable to convince herself that sexual love was not a sin. She had her mother to look after, but no other ties. There was the possibility of marriage, children even. Why not? Hopefully, Val would want the same.

The singing ended. The creaking pews became the loudest noise until the minister held up his hand like a traffic warden to give the valedictory benediction. At the signal word Amen the organ started playing again and he set off down the aisle to place himself four-square in the doorway to shake hands with each of his departing audience in turn. Only those right at the back had the opportunity to escape before he got into position. Everybody else had to wait in the slowly shuffling queue.

Maureen waited with the rest, not joining in the small talk, telling herself that her intended lover was not trying to avoid her and that there would be a simple explanation for his absence. He was not the only person missing from the church, after all. Gregor Runciman, Val's partner in the law firm, wasn't there either. And Zena McElhose, occupier of a pew right at the front, was another regular attender conspicuous by her absence. The firm handled her investments and business affairs. Val often spoke of her in affectionate terms, but Maureen had presumed it was because she was such a valuable client. Mrs McElhose was a widow, much older than Maureen, of course, but reasonably well preserved. Old friends sometimes found they had a lot more in common than they realised. Was it just a coincidence she and Val weren't at church? Maureen and Mrs McElhose were both on the flower-arranging rota for the church. Sometimes, for major services at Christmas and Easter, they worked together. They didn't speak much. They didn't have much in common. Perhaps Val had turned to her for comfort in his widowhood. Perhaps they were lying in bed together at that very moment, caressing each other, kissing, touching. Maureen closed her eyes and tried to force the image out of her mind but it wouldn't go. Jealousy made the muscles in her thighs twitch.

'Ah, Miss Gilliland. I hope you are well.'

The minister was holding Maureen's hand in both of his, rubbing it gently. Close up his round face, speckled with tiny blood vessels behind the beard, came into sharp focus. She regretted putting on too much lipstick and eye make-up and dyeing her hair. He must surely notice and suspect her true motivation. He was probably thinking what a brazen hussy she was.

'You are looking very well this morning, Miss Gilliland. You must let me in on whatever secret it is you have.'

Was he speaking in code? Did he really know what she was thinking? Did he know about Valentine and Zena's secret affair? Was he mocking her? Maureen muttered something non-committal and hurried past him out into the pale daylight with its watery threat of rain in the air. She went straight to her car, taking off her hat so that the brim didn't scrape the roof and exchanging her reading glasses for the pair she used for driving. She drove away from the church, feeling her courage dwindle as she did so, knowing that she would no longer have the courage to be sexually assertive if she saw Val coming towards her.

She doubled back and drove past the entrance to his house. There was no sign of life. The garage door was closed, the curtains open at all the windows. She should have been in there, engaged in sinful pleasure, but she wasn't. Maybe she had been saved from herself. Maybe not. Or maybe Val was ill. Should she go up and knock on the door? What would she say then if he answered? She would say she had been concerned about him. She would say she had missed him at the church. That was respectable. That was friendly. No one could take that amiss.

After five or six passes, Maureen steeled herself sufficiently to park her car in the street and walk up to the door. She rang the bell and listened to its hollow ringing resonate inside. There was no one at home. He must be with Zena. Where else could he be? She had no choice but to turn away, her whole body prickling with a combination of relief, frustration, and jealousy. She sat in her car and wiped off her lipstick with a tissue, glaring impotently at the red stain it made. Tears built up behind her eyes and forced themselves out. Everything around her was transformed into one amorphous blur. She removed her glasses and lowered her head. The tears began to drop from the point of her nose on to her hands.

10

Sunday, 12.43
A seven iron again. David Fyfe had decided what club to use before he walked up to his ball on the edge of the fairway and went through the rigmarole of estimating distance and tossing some grass in the air to check the wind strength. The seven iron was always the club he used when he managed to land on a fairway. He was comfortable with it, confident he could at the very least make decent contact between club head and ball and move it forward in the desired direction. He didn't want to start getting too smart now and worry overmuch about the subtler nuances of the game. He was striding down the eighteenth fairway at Gleneagles, one up with one to play. His drive had been left of the trees. His second an arrow-straight seven iron leaving him with a simple one hundred yard approach shot to the green ahead. He would take the seven once more. It was too much club but he would hold back a bit. He had never before won a tie at the challenge outing. Whatever happened he

couldn't lose but he wanted to win. This was his best chance. Dun Roamin, the hole was called. 'Don't blow it now,' he kept repeating to himself. 'Don't blow it now.'

On the right side of the fairway Eric Bradley was up to his knees in the rough, cursing under his breath as he tried to find a firm stance in the damp grass. Bradley had changed from his normal happy-go-lucky self on the back nine as his game had collapsed about him. Five up at the turn he was now one behind and in a foul mood. It was not because Fyfe had played particularly well, just steadily. He had achieved only one hole in par in the entire round, but it had been at the sixteenth, Lochan Loup, the hardest hole on the course, and it had been a real sickener for Bradley when the ball soared over the water in front of the green and rolled to within ten feet of the flag. Bradley's early run of three birdies in a row on the front nine had him jumping in the air and clicking his heels but it had been cancelled out by another run when he couldn't get below seven strokes a hole. That was when the clubs started to be slammed into the turf. By contrast Fyfe enjoyed the Perthshire scenery, regarding his sclaffed drives and fluffed chips with equanimity.

On the eighteenth fairway, Fyfe tapped the shafts of a few clubs and picked out his favourite seven iron. The day had grown sunnier and more pleasant. He had dispensed with his jacket at the sixth when he had lost his first ball, his jersey at the twelfth when another one went into trees never to be seen again.

He watched Bradley take a big swing and chew out a sheaf of grass. But the ball shot out of the rough, a daisy cutter never getting more than a foot above the ground. It bounced and rolled, missed the edge of a bunker by inches and trickled into the centre of the green.

'Ya beauty,' Bradley shouted after it.

'Shit,' Fyfe murmured, raising a hand to acknowledge a good shot even if it was down more to luck than judgement.

The pressure was on Fyfe. He had to get on the green to have a chance of winning now. He lined up, taking his time, rocking from foot to foot while he settled, flexing his wrists. Don't fuck up, he thought. Don't fuck up now.

He noticed Hilary's name and number written on the inside of his forearm. The sweat was making it fade rapidly. He had all but forgotten about her in the heat of head-to-head competition, but not quite. He had to win if he was going to phone her and get to see her in that little black dress again.

He swung the club. It moved smoothly, scooping the ball high into the air and dropping it perfectly on the green. It bounced three times and seemed to roll right up against the flagstick.

'Ya beauty,' Fyfe shouted after it, smiling over at Bradley as he raised a hand in acknowledgement.

They walked up to the green side by side. The foreshortening effect had fooled them. Fyfe's ball was at least twenty feet from the hole, and Bradley's only slightly closer. Fyfe sized up his putt, stalking round it and crouching down without really knowing what he was looking for. He decided to aim a few feet to the left, took a few practice swings and then set it on its way. It was right on line but not hard enough. It stopped eight inches from the hole. Fyfe picked it up and marked it, anticipating sinking it to confirm victory.

'This for the hole and to half the match,' Bradley said.

He putted. The ball rolled up the edge, hesitated, deliberated, sat back, changed its mind and dropped in. Fyfe sighed and shook hands magnanimously. He hadn't lost, so he reckoned that meant he could still phone Hilary if he wanted to. It was to be his decision.

They collected their bags from the fringe of the green and walked back to the club house discussing the what-might-have-beens and working out what was owed in cash and drink. Fyfe, it turned out, was in deficit in both. He thought back to a few flying divots, a bad shank at the Sleekit Howe tenth when his seven iron had let him down, and a couple of missed putts. If any one hadn't happened he would have won comfortably. But they had happened and he had neither won nor lost. A maroon-blazered steward met them at the door of the changing rooms and said that Sir Duncan wanted to see him as soon as possible. Fyfe changed his shirt and his socks and went up to the players' bar.

'How did you get on?' Sir Duncan asked.

'An honourable half,' Fyfe replied. 'And you?'

'I took the cocky bastard two and one. Were you planning to play again this afternoon?'

'Yes.'

'I'd be grateful if you didn't.'

37

Fyfe knew it wasn't so much a polite request as a subtle order. He couldn't refuse the chief. Well, he could, but he wouldn't. Not yet anyway, even though he had his own independent wealth stored away to compensate for any sudden loss of earnings. Sir Duncan, after rescuing Fyfe's career when he could have cut him off at the knees, liked to refer to him as his personal troubleshooter. More like his personal lackey, Fyfe thought regretfully.

'What's the problem?'

'I need you to go back to Edinburgh. I'd get Les to do it but his handicap is lower than yours and he's played really well this morning.'

From the bar Detective Superintendent Les Cooper smiled weakly across at Fyfe and lifted his glass of gin and tonic in a conciliatory wave.

'What's happened?' Fyfe asked.

'There's been a murder. We've only got Sapalski available to put on it. He's a bit inexperienced. I need you to mother hen him.'

'What's the story?'

'It's a nasty one, likely to attract a lot of media attention. Wealthy widow by the name of McElhose, pillar of the community, I'm told, lots of work for charity and that kind of thing. She was found dead in her kitchen this morning with her head bashed in.'

'Any suspects?'

'Bloke in combat gear lying unconscious in the front porch.'

'Alive?'

'Not dead. Unconscious.'

'And you're worried Sapalski won't ask him the obvious question?'

'The simplest cases often turn out to be the real bastards. You know that as well as anyone.' Sir Duncan packed tobacco into the bowl of his pipe and shook his head. 'I've got a bad feeling about this one. If this guy did it, who flattened him? I'd be happier if I knew you were on the case, Dave.'

Fyfe consulted his own sixth sense. An open and shut murder case that the greenest detective could solve without breaking sweat hardly seemed a good reason to abandon an annual afternoon on the luxurious fairways of Gleneagles. Sapalski,

38

known as the pedantic Pole, was a good professional. He wasn't likely to screw up badly in the space of a few hours. He would do the groundwork adequately. And yet there was a definite hint of a tremor there. Something not quite right.

'Combat gear, you say?'

'Overalls, balaclava and surgical gloves.'

'She disturbed him at it and suffered the consequences?'

'Maybe. I'd just feel happier if there was someone like you watching over the situation, Dave. I don't want this one to run out of control.'

'What was her name?'

'McElhose.' Sir Duncan consulted a scrap of paper torn from a notebook. 'Zena McElhose.'

'Zena?'

'Yes. It's not that uncommon a name.'

'Fairly unusual.'

'All right. It's fairly uncommon.'

The name clinched it for Fyfe. His sixth sense trembled like a pointer dog in front of a hidden grouse. Last night while he was eyeing up Hilary at the party it had been Zeno's paradox and here he was confronted out of the blue with the feminine version, Zena's paradox. Gleneagles' attractions paled. Somebody was trying to tell him something. He had to go.

Fyfe took his leave of the outing as the main body settled down to lunch in the restaurant. He consoled himself with the prospect that he would have probably had a much worse round in the afternoon, and hopefully that fate would now befall Super Cooper. As it was, the what-might-have-beens from it would never now be translated into more lost balls and missed putts because they would never happen.

He climbed into his car and drove out of the hotel grounds. A squeal of the tyres as he rounded the bend on to the main road emphasised his urgency. First he phoned Sapalski and got a rundown on the details as he negotiated the narrow twisting road north of Dunfermline. From what he was told it sounded pretty straightforward. Not much of a paradox at all. Of course, as Sir Duncan had already pointed out, that often turned out to be the worst kind of case. The mystery man was in hospital and the balaclava and the rest of his gear were in plastic evidence bags. That was as good a place to start as any. He rolled up his sleeve and reminded himself of Hilary's number. He punched it into the handset. It rang for a long time before it was answered. He was just going up the slope of the slip road on to the motorway.

'Hi there,' he said. 'Met any strange men at parties recently?'

'I can't talk now. I'll phone you back.'

It was short and didn't sound very sweet. Then she hung up. Fyfe didn't know if he should be aggrieved at her abrupt manner. He must have caught her at a bad moment. How was she going to phone him back? She didn't know his number, did she? The phone started to ring within minutes. Another paradox for him to work out, he thought. Hilary did know the number.

He left it for a few moments lest he appear too eager then unhooked the phone and put it to his ear. His tentative plan was to briefly babysit Sapalski, unmask Zena McElhose's murderer, accept the plaudits of a grateful public and still have time to take Hilary out on the town.

'Hello there, stranger,' a woman said. 'Remember me?'

A cavalry charge of memories galloped through Fyfe's mind at the sound of the familiar husky voice. Dead bodies, fresh blood, the crunch of glass underfoot, sackfuls of banknotes, warm flesh, wet lips, hot breath, scratching fingernails, fond farewells. Everything else was overwhelmed by the sudden drama of his past catching up with him.

He steered his car into a lay-by where lorries waited if the wind was too strong to cross the bridge. He didn't move from behind the wheel and he didn't say anything into the phone. He didn't know what to say. He didn't want to say anything that would antagonise her. He especially didn't want to do that. Nor did he want his silence to antagonise her either. Angela could be a dangerous lady to know, a very dangerous lady.

'Well, I asked a simple question,' Angela said. 'Do you remember me?'

Fyfe took a deep, slow breath.

'How could I forget?' he replied.

11

Sunday, 12.45

The slice of fruit cake was half-way to her mouth when Maureen Gilliland heard the news item on the radio. The significance didn't register until her teeth were closing on the cake. A woman found dead. Not yet named. Police treating the death as suspicious. Large detached house. Wardie Avenue. Somebody else taken from the house by ambulance. Not named. Condition unknown. Door-to-door inquiries. Frightened neighbours. Confusion. Consternation. Appeal for witnesses.

Zena McElhose lived in Wardie Avenue. There were only three or four big houses in Wardie Avenue, each in its own grounds overlooking the sea. Gilliland coughed, spraying cake crumbs into her lap. Neither Zena nor Val Randolph had been at church. He could be the other person taken away in the ambulance. Suppose they had been together, spent the night together, and there had been some kind of tremendous row. Supposing he had killed her in a fit of madness, and then tried to kill himself in a fit of remorse. Gilliland's whole body began to shiver, as though the temperature in the room had suddenly plummeted. It should have been her, she thought unwillingly. It should have been her. She had to get up and hurry to the bathroom to empty her bladder.

Her mother barely looked up from behind her barrier of newspapers when she shouted that she was going out to visit a friend. She was so nervous she had to hold her wrist with her free hand to control its shaking to be able to insert the key in the ignition of the car. The traffic was sparse, the city quiet. There were few people about as she drove to the north side, gripping the steering wheel far too tightly, braking far too heavily then accelerating awkwardly. The only station she could find on the radio that wasn't just music was a phone-in programme run by a presenter with an annoyingly superior tone in his voice and a stupid made-up name, Tam Spurious. But she was glad of something to occupy her mind. A fast-moving succession of people offering their opinions was ridiculed and insulted by him. An occasional catchy jingle said the show was live and not subject to any time delay. That was its gimmick. Callers were put straight on the air. Anything could happen.

'I just think it's terrible, so I do, the way this government's ruining this country,' said one earnest caller.

'Well, that will have them quaking in their brown suede shoes and Italian suits inside the Mother of Parliaments tonight,' answered Spurious facetiously. 'People like you always complain but you never do anything about it. Stop whining and start acting. Next caller, please.'

'I want to talk about the state of the health service.'

'No chance, but if they ever introduce euthanasia I'm sure they'll call on you to bore the bastards to death. Next caller.'

'I think you're very rude, Mr Spurious.'

'Don't let me disappoint you then. Piss off. Next caller, please.'

'Fucking brainless – '

The torrent of expletives was cut off after only two words by a blast of loud rock music.

'My, my,' said Spurious. 'Engineer Rodney's on the ball to protect my delicate ears today. Keep the calls coming, folks, but keep them clean. I'm here this afternoon and evening. We never close. Anything you want to tell me. Anything you want to get off your chest. Let's share it with everybody out there. Remember we're not alone. And now a message from our sponsors so you poor suckers can waste your cash.'

The advertisements began as Gilliland turned the car into Wardie Avenue. She reached down without looking and put off the radio. The big houses were all behind high walls overhung by huge trees. Clumps of wet leaves clogged the pavements. There was nothing to be seen as she approached the entrance to Zena McElhose's house. A strange sensation of disappointment settled over her. It was a childish thing, like when she was young and opening a present to find something she didn't really want inside, and having to pretend that it didn't matter.

Then she saw the policeman. The black coat, silver markings on the epaulettes, white shirt collar, the cap with black and white squared strip. He was standing by the gate, half hidden, looking down intently at his feet as he tried to scrape a leaf from the surface of the ground with the toe of his shoe. And behind him in the driveway was one orange and white police car, with another less colourful car beyond it. And there was a caravan with the police coat of arms on it and a shutter propped open at the window as though it should be selling tea and hot dogs. Another man in plain clothes was walking to the door of the lodge where the curtains were closed.

Gilliland drove past, suddenly excited, sitting erect. The policeman at the gate lifted his head and glanced at her but without any particular interest. He began to punch one black-gloved fist into the palm of the other hand.

It was Zena then, Gilliland was thinking. Did that mean it was Val too? The buzz of vicarious excitement, fear and envy all entwined made her vision blur slightly. She gripped the steering wheel even tighter and turned the corner at the end of the avenue. A row of terraced houses stood back on one side while on the other the land fell away abruptly, giving an uninterrupted view out over a spread of low rooftops to the broad estuary. The tide was in. The water was high. Gilliland's bladder was full again. She needed to go to the bathroom.

She almost collided with the little white car, parked in isolation on the opposite side of the street to every other vehicle. She slammed on the brakes at the last moment. The seat belt tightened across her chest, squeezing her ribs uncomfortably. Her head snapped forward. Her car slid on the greasy roadway but stopped with room to spare. She breathed deeply and composed herself. She took off her glasses and rubbed them clean. When she replaced them the white car sprang into sudden focus. She read the number plate and recoiled from the familiarity. It was Val's car, the runabout he used when his big red Mercedes was being serviced or the weather was particularly bad. Here it was, parked beside Zena McElhose's house where the police were investigating a murder. She had been right. All this time it had been the two of them. There was something she expected inside the invisible present after all. She had expected it but she didn't want it. She started to cry.

Gilliland manoeuvred round Val's little car, looking anxiously in the mirror to check that the police weren't following her. It was only once she had driven several hundred yards away that she became aware of the warmth round her thighs gradually turning cold. She had wet herself.

43

12

John Sapalski could not take his eyes off the little girl curled in her mother's lap. She was staring out at him with huge brown eyes. Her skin was chalk white. She looked incredibly delicate, as if capable of shattering in pieces at the slightest touch, but there was life shining inside her like the burning filament inside an opaque electric bulb. The plastic apparatus attached to the little girl's discoloured forearm hung like a parasite sucking the blood and the energy and the life from her.

'It took us a long time to come to terms with Lorna's condition,' Marianne Dunne was saying. 'She's had one bone marrow transplant and it didn't take. She's had every conceivable drug treatment. Nothing worked and she was in a lot of pain. Eventually, we decided enough was enough and brought her home. At least she's not in much pain any more as long as we keep her topped up. And she looks better now that her hair has grown back. Now it's just like it was when she was a baby.'

Marianne gently stroked her daughter's fine hair. Sapalski didn't say anything. She looked like a baby to him. He was frightened he would be too emotional to make any sense. He was thinking about the complex biological process forming his own baby inside his wife's womb, wondering if something might have already gone wrong that they wouldn't know for years.

'Sandy took it harder than me. It was a male thing, I suppose, being unable to protect his daughter against the invisible enemy inside. He drank for a while, but then he got over that. He's all right even though it still hurts. He's accepted it now, thank God. He's much calmer.'

Sapalski wondered how he could steer the conversation round to the subject of a very dead Zena McElhose. What did he say; that he didn't care about the girl, that he wasn't interested in whether she lived or died, that he only wanted to talk about death? His child might be a daughter. He had seen the blurred image on the screen of the ultrasound machine at the clinic. If it was a girl, she might be born and then die just as this little girl was going to. How would he handle those circumstances? How would he feel if his own child stared at him with big questioning eyes and innocently asked what was happening to her and why didn't he do something to help her?

'The doctors tried everything,' Marianne repeated. 'They can't say for sure but she's probably got about six months left. That's why I never leave her for long. The drug doses just kill the pain now. They're not fighting the cancer itself any more. It was too much for Lorna. Her hair fell out, her gums were bleeding, all the usual sort of things. It was killing her. Literally. But there's always hope, isn't there? Miracles have been known to happen. We're patiently waiting for one to happen to us.'

'Marianne,' Sapalski said. 'May I call you Marianne?'

'Of course you may.' She sat rocking slightly with her arms wrapped loosely round her child, smiling faintly. Would he take it so well if he was in her position? Pin-points of light reflected on the pupils of the little girl's glossy brown eyes.

'I'm sorry to have to bother you, Marianne, but I really do have to ask about Mrs McElhose.'

He gestured back over his shoulder with a clumsy flick of his head, meaning to indicate the big house at the end of the drive. He didn't want to mention death or dead bodies while Lorna was looking at him so intensely. The words would have stuck in his throat.

'I understand.'

'I know you've already done it for another officer but can you just tell me in your own words how you came to find Mrs McElhose?'

'Certainly.'

She told him, explaining the sequence of events in coherent sentences that left nothing out. She showed him the cuts on the soles of her feet now covered with sticking plasters. She was so relaxed sitting there with her dying daughter clinging to her and watching the stranger anxiously. There was a serenity about the mother, Sapalski thought. It was suggestive of sainthood or martyrdom. She would probably have gone through an angry phase, then suicidal, then maybe apathetic. And here she was in front of him, still waiting, perhaps still changing. How many more phases might there be?

45

'Did Mrs McElhose have many friends?'

'Not a huge number. She was a church member. Sometimes people would come back for afternoon tea. Not often. She liked her own company mostly.'

'Family?'

'Spread to the four winds. They kept in touch. Regular letters and phone calls. She used to visit them quite a lot. They're being informed, your colleague said. A granddaughter lives in London. Her name is Carole, I think.'

'She was a widow?'

'Yes.'

'Long?'

'As long as we've been here and that's five years now, before Lorna was born.'

'How old was she?'

'Over seventy, I think.'

'Did she have any . . .'

Sapalski struggled to find an alternative description for boyfriends. It seemed completely inappropriate to talk about boyfriends and a woman of seventy. Lorna made a tiny mewing sound, like an injured kitten. Sapalski wanted to reach out and comfort her. Her mother glanced down fondly and began to rock her animatedly.

'Do you mean were there any gentlemen callers?' she said.

'Exactly.'

'No. I don't think so anyway. I only did breakfast for her and the cleaning, but I would have seen the cars go up the drive. No, she was the epitome of respectability. There was the minister but he doesn't count, does he?'

Sapalski laughed with her and imagined he saw the ghost of a smile flit across little Lorna's face.

'I doubt it,' he said. 'Doesn't leave us much to go on.'

'What about the man behind the front door?'

Sapalski shook his head. In the model investigative scenario, she wouldn't have known what he knew about the man behind the door. But she had seen the ambulance, of course, and she had been allowed to talk to her husband Sandy who had been with Sapalski when they found him. Ideally, they should have been kept apart until separate statements had been taken from them. He should have engineered that but it was too late now.

She hadn't been aware of the stranger before Sandy told her, she said.

'Any idea who he is?' he asked.

'None. Have you?'

'A housebreaker?'

'Are balaclava and overalls not a bit melodramatic for a simple thief?'

'An over-dressed housebreaker disturbed in the act,' Sapalski suggested.

'Why did he kill her then?'

'Panic. He didn't mean to. She was old and frail. The blow wouldn't have killed a younger, stronger person.'

'And who knocked him out?'

'His partner? Or he was alone and fell and hit his head in the scramble to escape? Have there been any other housebreakings in this area recently?'

'I don't think so.'

'I'll check that.'

Lorna coughed and her entire little body trembled with the aftershock. Her eyes blinked slowly and then she was watching Sapalski once more. He noticed a darker patch of skin on the contour of her jawbone and wondered if it was caused by the cancer inside her.

'If that's all, Inspector, I'll put Lorna to bed. She likes me to lie down with her until she falls asleep. I like it too.'

Sapalski stood up as Marianne left the room. He felt guilty that he was glad she was going, glad he didn't have to look at the dying child any longer. She was really getting to him. He had written hardly anything in his notebook, just a series of unfinished sentences and meaningless doodles. He was reminding himself to phone his pregnant wife and ask how she was when Sandy Ramensky was shown in for the next interview session.

13

David Fyfe's parked car rocked in the sudden slipstream of an articulated lorry that was travelling too fast as it came into the lay-by. The wheels locked and squealed, skidding on the greasy surface, spitting out little chips of stones. Black marks appeared behind it on the tarmac, like fingers clawing to prevent it going over the edge. The sound rose to a crescendo and then stopped abruptly. The lorry came to a halt, its line broken by the obtuse angle of the beginning of a jack-knife. The air brakes gasped. Vapour rose from the tyres, accumulating in the wheel arches and then sliding up the grey canvas sides blazoned in huge red lettering with the legend *Steady, Safe and Sure* pierced by a yellow bolt of lightning.

'What on earth was that?' Angela asked over the phone.

'Nothing really,' Fyfe replied. 'An accident that didn't happen.'

'Where are you?'

'On the motorway.'

'Am I distracting you?'

'Not in the least,' he lied.

'Times have changed then.'

Fyfe regained a little of the composure that had deserted him when Angela's voice had so unexpectedly invaded the car. He was, he told himself, confident he could handle this latest complication in his life. He had it all sussed out. Angela, his partner in crime, had as much to lose as him so she wouldn't make trouble. She was the scorpion and he was the fox swimming across the river, each dependent on the other as the old proverb said. Only in the proverb the scorpion stung the fox. Why did you do it, the fox asked? Because it's my nature, the scorpion said. And they both drowned.

'So we'll have lunch then?' Angela said.

'If I can get away.'

'You'll get away.' The way she said it, it sounded like an order. 'You can't stand up an old friend, an old lover.'

'I'll do my best.'

'What? To stand me up?'

'You know what I mean.'

'Good, better, best. Never let it rest, till your good is better and your better's best. It's a rhyme I learned at my old primary school. Funny how you remember things like that, isn't it?'

'Yeah. Funny.'

Fyfe remembered all sorts of things about Angela. They went a long way back. He had first met her to inform her of the untimely death of her husband, an armed robber called Mad Mike Barrie who preferred to blow his own head off and incinerate more than one million pounds in used notes rather than surrender to the police. One thing led to another and, since Fyfe was going through a difficult episode with his wife Sally at the time, he and Angela ended up consoling each other in the biblical, not the professional sense. That had been the first time, a time so far in the distance he thought of it in black and white rather than Technicolor.

Fast forward to almost a decade later when Barrie's sidekick, John Adamson, the one without the death wish, got out of prison and Barrie's big-time brother decided the cash hadn't gone up in smoke and went looking for him so that he could return it to Angela, the grieving widow, and have her say thank you very much. And then there was Fyfe stumbling across this situation, in among the glittering shards of shattered glass and the stiffening of dying bodies and blood blooms floating sedately in a swimming pool like underwater cumulus clouds. There he came face to face with Angela for the second time, standing beside a pile of black plastic bags stuffed with used banknotes. He remembered she was wearing exactly the same kind of short black figure-hugging dress that Hilary had worn at the party only the night before when his head was trying to get round Zeno's paradoxes and old Zena whatshername was being murdered elsewhere to add an extra dimension of intrigue to the riddle. Funny how things that happened around him always seemed to fit into some kind of weird, incomprehensible pattern.

Anyway, it was just over a year since he had done his duty, turned Angela and the money in, written up his report and lived happily ever after. Except, ever the sucker for a damsel in distress, he had done the opposite. His dogs, not even born when

49

he had first comforted Angela, had taken kindly to her so she couldn't be all bad. He had hurried her and the money away from the scene of carnage, then slept with her to confirm her innocence of involvement in murder and his own weakness for carnality at moments of stress. And he had sent her on her way at dead of night on the sleeper in the direction of Europe. In return she had given him one of the suitcases full of cash, the great bulk of which he still had hidden in biscuit boxes under the floor of his garden shed. Bloody hell, talk about a night to remember.

Now Angela was back in his life for the third time, whispering in his ear while he sat at the side of a busy motorway and in front of him the driver of an almost out of control articulated lorry kicked a smoking tyre. Fyfe switched on the air conditioning to keep out the smell of burning rubber. Good things always came in threes, he thought. And bad things.

'My treat,' Angela said. 'At the Caledonian. One o'clock.'

'You're not short of a bob or two then? I mean, it's not cheap at the Caley.'

'Did you ever know me to worry about money?'

Fyfe had tried to raise the subject of money with subtlety, but knew he had failed. Now they were both thinking about the weight of those notes straining the plastic of the bags and the sound of the glass being crushed under the soles of their shoes so they had to pick out the specks like bits of silvery grit. Did she want her money back?

'Where are you just now, Angela?'

'I'm in London. A posh hotel in Park Lane. Nothing but the best for me these days.'

'What are you doing with yourself?'

'The usual. By the way, I'm a wife again.'

'Congratulations. How many times is that?'

'Fourth, I think. Or it might be fifth. It's easy to lose count.'

'Who's the lucky man?'

'Felippe. He's a widower, has a big estate near Barcelona and he's a member of the European Parliament.'

'Sounds cosy.'

'It is.'

'So what are you doing over here?'

'I'm with Felippe. We're part of an official delegation investigating tourist facilities in various countries. It's just a single day in Edinburgh. We're flying up on the last shuttle tonight but I can't get out of the dinner. Besides, I want to look my best for you, David darling. By tomorrow I'll be all rested and much better company.'

'Just one day here. Are you sure you can fit me in?'

'Definitely. You have special dispensation. I would be extremely upset if we missed each other.'

Was it a threat? Was she warning him that if he stood her up she would expose him? But then she was guilty too. Was she coming back to reclaim the money she had given him? Was this blackmail?

'So tell me what you are doing with yourself.'

'I'm investigating a murder.'

'A nice juicy one?'

'I don't know yet. You interrupted me on my way to view the battered corpse.'

'We seem to make a habit of meeting while people are dropping dead around us.'

It was the first direct reference to the circumstances of their last meeting. The implication of it buzzed in the short silence that followed. They were the only two people in the world who knew their secret. He pictured Angela's astonished eyes staring at him when he had found her beside the swimming pool surrounded by the dead and dying. Then the eyes had been pleading for his help. He wondered what he would see in them now.

'Is that good or bad?' he asked.

'Depends who's dropping dead.'

'As long as it's not us.'

'You and I are survivors, David.'

'So far, anyway.'

'Look, I've got to go. Felippe's calling me. See you tomorrow. Don't be late. Good luck with your murder.'

She was gone before he could say anything else. He was left staring out from the purple car he had bought with a small handful of his stolen money. Tiny pin-points of rain were appearing at widely spaced intervals on the glass of the windscreen. He tried to find some pattern in their arrangement but knew full well it would make no sense.

51

14

Ramensky seemed almost too big for the armchair. He sat awkwardly hunched up with his elbows on his knees and his knuckles pressed together in front of his mouth. He looked over at Sapalski the way his daughter Lorna had, except his eyes were older, wiser, wilier. The skin around them was creased and wrinkled. Underneath hung dark crescent shadows like pencil marks. There was yellow nicotine staining on his fingers but he didn't produce any cigarettes. Sapalski listened to his story, thinking that he couldn't trust anything this man told him.

'So that's it, you've no idea who our friend by the front door is?'

'No idea at all,' Ramensky replied, his words muffled behind his fists.

'Or how he got in?'

'Through a window somewhere, I suppose.'

'The house has a fairly elaborate alarm system. How would he manage that?'

'Don't know. Nothing's perfect, is it? Maybe he found the key under the frog?'

'Maybe somebody told him where it was?'

'Maybe.'

'Have there ever been break-ins before?'

'No.'

Sapalski focused his thoughts on the alarm system because he hadn't considered it before. Now he remembered there was a complicated box of tricks inside the back door. It must have cost a lot, yet these things were easily bypassed by the use of shaving foam and the like if you knew where to squirt it. A cursory inspection of the property had found no sign of any forced entry. The back door key was still under the stone frog. It could have been used to unlock the door and then replaced. Or could old Zena have let her murderer in willingly? Unlikely, given that he was wearing a balaclava, or maybe they were lovers into kinky

52

sex games? At her age? Surely not? The key under the frog was favourite.

'It's ironic, don't you agree, Inspector?' Ramensky said, dropping his hands from his face.

'What is?'

'Mrs McElhose's death.'

'Ironic? In what way?'

'Well, she was old and probably didn't have very long to go anyway. Then there's Lorna, who is so young and has her whole life in front of her. Yet she's going to die soon. And here they were, the old and the young, living within a few hundred yards of each other. Don't you think that's somehow ironic?'

Sapalski didn't answer. He couldn't think of anything appropriate to say. Yes, it was cruelly ironic. Yes, he thought, it's Sod's law all right. And he blushed because he wanted to say he was sorry but knew just how futile that would sound. Ramensky was no longer looking at him but right through him.

'When I think about it, I sometimes wonder if it would have been possible to transfer some of her life into Lorna,' Ramensky said. 'Not just hers, not just Mrs McElhose, but anybody. There are all these people going about who don't need it all. Me, for example. Why can't I just hand over some of my life to my little daughter? I would willingly. I desperately want to but I can't. I thought about it for a long time and I almost convinced myself I was on to something. It was like when you try to remember something, a name or a place, and it's a complete blank but you know it's there, you know it will come to you eventually. That was what I thought for a long time, that the secret to save Lorna would suddenly come to me and it would be so simple and straightforward I wouldn't be able to understand why I hadn't thought of it before.'

Ramensky paused, staring into space. His eyes were pink, pupils gaping black. The chair his large frame was perched on looked like a piece of doll's furniture behind him. Where Marianne had been serene, Ramensky was angry and bitter. Sapalski sensed the repressed violence emanating from him and it wasn't a great leap of the imagination to be able to picture him killing Mrs McElhose, lashing out because he believed through warped logic that her death would help his daughter live. It was a motive of sorts. 'I'm a big man, a powerful man, as you can see,' Ramensky said. 'I take after my father. He was second generation. My grandfather came across in 1938 to settle here. I've still got relatives in Poland though I've never been across. Never felt the urge.' He stopped talking, cutting himself off in mid-sentence then beginning again a few moments later. 'When you're big you don't feel threatened by many things. People don't bother you because they know that if they do they'll come off second best. You always feel you can cope no matter what. That was how I felt all my life. And I've been healthy. I'm never ill. So here I am now, a big man and I can't do a thing to save the life of my baby daughter. All my size, all my strength isn't worth as much as a fart in a thunderstorm.'

Sapalski's grandfather had settled in Scotland during the war too, confirming a tenuous link between the two men. Sapalski had never been to Poland either and the only time he had contemplated going was when a romantic notion overwhelmed him during the time of Solidarnosc and Lech Walesa. It had quickly passed. An aged uncle in a village outside Warsaw wrote to him twice a year in fractured English informing him of the continuing history of an extended family he had never met. He had a pile of fading photographs detailing the history of strangers. He and Ramensky would have had more in common if Sapalski was six inches taller and weighed five stone more.

Ramensky was suddenly grimacing horribly. His body tensed and stiffened, elongating. The cords round his neck muscles bulged alarmingly. He almost bared his teeth. Sapalski thought he was either suffering a heart attack or he was about to burst into tears. He watched in hypnotic fascination, half rising to go to his aid but unsure what he could do.

When Ramensky broke wind it rasped loudly like a piece of cloth being ripped in two. The springs of the chair below him resonated like a distant trumpet voluntary. Then his whole body relaxed as abruptly as it had tensed. His habitual hangdog expression returned.

'You imagine all sorts of things,' Ramensky continued. 'If my grandfather had stayed in Poland he would never have met my grandmother Macdonald and I would never have been born. Therefore Lorna would never have been born. Therefore she wouldn't have to die so young. That would solve the immediate problem, wouldn't it?'

54

Sapalski decided to stop indulging the big man and get on with the job. Again, he noticed with annoyance, his notebook was filled mainly with doodles instead of writing. It didn't matter. Both husband and wife would make and sign formal statements. The task had already been delegated. Sapalski could go home to his wife, but first he had to make contact with Chief Inspector Fyfe, sent back from the annual golf outing to watch over him. Fyfe was sure to be in a bad temper because of that, so Sapalski wanted to have every angle covered so there was nothing for him to complain about.

'Sandy, did you kill Mrs McElhose?' he asked.

Ramensky's mind returned from its rambling excursion into his personal philosophy. He saw Sapalski opposite him as though surprised to find him there. He balled his fists and touched knuckles in front of his mouth then rubbed them hard into his eye sockets.

'Do you know who did kill her?' Sapalski asked.

There was more hesitation. Ramensky spread his fingers over his face, smoothing the skin, pulling his eyes out of shape to give himself a sinister Oriental-style look. Was he deliberately delaying? Did he know more than he let on? Sapalski couldn't fathom him at all.

'I reckon you'll find out sooner or later,' Ramensky said.

'Find out what?'

'Who killed her.'

'We usually do.'

Ramensky sat back in the chair, squeezed tight between its arms. 'It wasn't necessary,' he said. 'To kill her, I mean.'

'What do you mean, not necessary?'

'She was old. She didn't have much life left.'

'That doesn't mean she deserved to die.'

Ramensky's wide shoulders rose and fell in a gesture of total defeatism. 'Everything has its season. You live, you die. We've all got to die sometime, haven't we?' he said.

15

Sunday, 13.48
The bunch of keys was heavy, a solid weight dangling by its chain from finger and thumb. It rotated slowly, making the light move across the silver and brass. Maureen Gilliland sat at the dressing-table in her bedroom, trying to hypnotise herself with the keys so that she wouldn't be afraid of what she had decided to do next. She didn't hear the shuffling footsteps or the knock at the door. The voice cut through her concentration though, making her snatch the keys into her closed hand to hide them.

'Are you all right in there, Maureen?'

'Fine, Mum.'

'Are you sure? You're not looking well today.'

'I'm okay.'

'I don't want an invalid on my hands.'

'Don't worry. I'll be out to make the tea in a moment.'

'I'll just go back and read my book then.'

'You do that.'

Gilliland listened to her mother shuffling away. She should have left home a long time ago, but it had never happened. She had been plagued by boyfriends when she was a teenager but had always remained coy and aloof. Then, suddenly, she was older and there were no boys interested in her any more and a future of barren loneliness stretched into the distance ahead of her. She retreated into a hard-skinned shell, covering all the mirrors in her room so that she didn't have to look at herself. That way she was able to retain her own exclusive self-image as a youngster, ignoring the constant glimpses of a totally different person she saw reflected in shop windows or the metallic paint of parked cars. In this guise, she admired her idol Valentine from afar. Before his recent conversion to physical displays he had kissed her twice a year, at Christmas and on her birthday. For weeks beforehand every nerve-ending tingled with keen anticipation of the touch of his lips against her cheek. But she never responded other than with a shy smile, confining her claim on him to shocking night-time fantasies that left her breathless and ashamed at the degeneracy of her imagination.

Never once in twenty years did she give Val any cause to suspect her secret longing for him. Out of consideration for his wife Joan, who was also a member of St Andrew's Church and of the flower-arranging committee, she never flirted, never imagined she would ever act inappropriately. But then Joan died and Val was available even if she was unable to think of it as anything but adultery. He certainly changed after the funeral, becoming alternately more distant and introverted, and outgoing and gregarious. He was obviously contemplating the same lonely future that Gilliland had been resigned to. On her last birthday he was slightly tipsy when he put his arm round her waist and kissed her hard on the lips, pressing the entire length of his body against hers. She had to rush to the bathroom and douse her face in cold water.

She was patient, not wanting to spoil things by adopting too presumptuous an attitude. She bided her time, judging the moment when she would make her declaration. The moment should have been today. And she discovered that he had been having a torrid affair with Zena McElhose. Not a young girl, but Zena, who limped around on her artificial hip and who was thirty years older than Gilliland.

She opened her fist. She had been squeezing the bunch of keys tightly and the marks of their teeth were deeply indented into her skin. It was her own fault that she had been betrayed. She should have announced her feelings much earlier. She should have comforted Val openly after Joan's death, instead of settling for a chaste handshake at the crematorium. She stared into the rumpled surface of the sheet draped over the arched mirror in front of her. Too late now, she thought. Too late now.

The keys in her hand were the spare set Valentine kept. He had never told her why he carried such a varied set of keys or why there were so many. On the one occasion she had asked, he had just given her one of those confidential winks he always used when they talked about the big fee-paying clients. Now she knew. One of these keys presumably gave him access to Zena McElhose's house. Others would be for other women. He had been doing it deliberately to taunt her.

Gilliland's love for Val was being transformed into hate. She

57

could feel it inside her, twisting and shrivelling like a piece of burning paper. She wanted to hurt Val, to damage him, to cause him to feel the same sort of pain she was now experiencing. He deserved it.

But first she had to make her mother's tea.

16

Sunday, 14.11

David Fyfe stood in the room in the intensive care unit at Edinburgh Royal Infirmary surrounded by bleeping technology and watched a nurse run through a check list, consulting monitor screens rather than the wired-up patient lying prone on the bed with a butterfly-wing plaster like a Maltese Cross stuck to his forehead. The door opened and a young baby-faced doctor in a starched white coat entered. Fyfe recognised him but struggled for a name. McInnes, it said on his badge. Dr Ken McInnes, that was it. They had had dealings before. His hair was shorter, receding badly from prominent temples and a smooth-skinned brow. A stethoscope hung round his neck like a skinny pet snake.

'Well, well, Chief Inspector, another day, another mystery.'

'Good morning, doctor. How are you hanging?'

'Swinging low as usual.'

'Lost any patients recently?'

'I'm up to quota. Good to see you've brought me a live one. You provided mainly stiffs in the past, if I remember correctly. Not a great deal even a talented medicine man like myself can do once the spark has been extinguished.'

'So what about this one?' Fyfe said, nodding towards the bed. 'What are his chances?'

'Reasonably good as we approach the Millennium. Back in the nineteenth century they would probably have planted him long ago. Now, however, we strive officiously to keep them ticking over. Science is a wonderful thing.'

'What happened to him?'

'In my professional opinion he suffered a myocardial infarction which rendered him temporarily unconscious causing him to fall over and inflict on himself the head injury you see here.'

'He had a heart attack and fell over?'

'Precisely.'

'Are you sure about that?'

'Absolutely. I will swear to it in a court of law too, if you make it worth my while.'

'You're pretty smart, Dr McInnes.'

'Thank you for the compliment, Chief Inspector Forbes.'

'Fyfe.'

'Chief Inspector Fyfe.'

'That's okay. It's been a while since we did our last body, and I don't go around with a name badge.'

'No name for our pal here, I see.'

'No name badge for him either. If he did, it would make our job a lot easier.'

'We call him John Doe. A bit of an Americanism, I realise, but we are living in the global village. All the tags were cut out of the clothes he was admitted in. Nothing in his pockets to identify him. Do you reckon he's got something to hide?'

'Possibly.'

'Did he bump off the old lady?'

'Possibly.'

'Poor bastard maybe doesn't want to wake up then?'

'Who can tell?'

The nurse had gone. They were standing on opposite sides of the ICU bed. McInnes used a thumb to open the patient's eyelid and shone a pencil-thin beam of light into the pupil. Then he turned round and studied one of the head-high screens, tracing the line with the fingers of one hand while he picked at spots on his face with the other.

'How can you tell it was a heart attack?' Fyfe asked.

'Oh good, I get to blind you with science,' McInnes replied.

'Go on then.'

'The electrical activity of the heart muscle can be recorded by an electrocardiograph like this one here. You see, the heart works like an electrical capacitor. Its normal pattern is to polarise and then depolarise, but in somebody suffering an infarction the rhythm is interrupted. It can be triggered by a number of things, bad diet, bad lifestyle, stress, over-excitement. And it generally happens over a number of days and finally it gets too much and the guy keels over. If a particular segment of an ECG is abnormal it evolves into what we call Q-waves, that hopefully don't exist for healthy folk like you and me, although you being of a certain age are more at risk than me.'

'So you can detect a heart attack before it happens.'

'If people came in for an ECG every morning. But life's not like that.'

Fyfe surreptitiously rubbed his hand over his heart, wondering what his personal ECG pattern would look like when he came face to face with Angela the next day. Stress, excitement, bad lifestyle. All the warning signs were there. McInnes yawned ostentatiously and flicked at his shirt collar.

'I won't bore you with an explanation of P-waves and T-waves and the QRS complex. No, basically our pal got a blast of his own mortality when his pump shut off the oxygen to his brain momentarily and down he went, bashing his head on the way.'

'Will he survive?'

'He would if it was just his heart. If he gets past the first few days there is an excellent survival rate six months after the event although after three years they're dropping like flies. The head injury here is a distorting factor for evaluation purposes.'

'Come on, medicine man, don't fail me now.'

'Science isn't good at predicting the effect of a blow to the head. For John Doe, it might mean nothing worse than a mild headache. Or it might mean he's as good as dead.'

'Bad as that?'

'There's evidence of a small leakage of blood into the skull cavity. Not significant at this stage but a leak's a leak. It could be worse, but it could be better. I've seen worse head trauma and total recovery. I've seen less apparently serious trauma and they end up lying in the cabbage patch upstairs.' He raised his eyebrows. 'The neurological trauma ward. We keep it in the attick so as not to frighten folks still functioning.'

'Is our John Doe going to come round?'

'Who knows?'

'As you say, maybe he doesn't want to?'

'Aha, so he did kill the old lady then.'

Fyfe was reluctant to condemn the unconscious man but didn't see much alternative. If the fall had knocked him out that ruled out a third party and left him all alone. He looked relatively harmless lying on his back with his double chins puckered up, his bushy eyebrows, and his chest smeared with Vaseline to improve the contact of the electrodes.

'The will to live is an important factor in these cases,' McInnes said rather pompously.

'What about the desire to die?'

'That too.'

'So what are you telling me, doctor?'

'What do you want to hear?'

'What would you tell his nearest and dearest?'

'There is every chance of full recovery but you must be prepared for the possibility of death or brain damage and a continuous state of coma. Be optimistic but I don't want to mislead you in any way.'

'And me? What would you tell me? Does he live or die?'

'One or the other.'

'Which?'

'If it was a horse race I wouldn't bet on him. That's not scientific by the way, that's a gut feeling.'

'Thanks for the diagnosis.'

'Any time. That will be twenty-five guineas, please.'

'Here's my card. Call me if he reaches re-entry stage.'

Sapalski barged in at that moment, apologising for not arriving earlier, breathing heavily after running up the flights of stairs because he was more concerned with haste than dignity having said he would be at the hospital to meet Fyfe. He shook hands with Fyfe and stretched across John Doe to do the same with McInnes.

A stern-looking nurse with eyelashes like spider legs came in after him and stood at the end of the bed with her arms folded. She said something unintelligible to McInnes, turned on her heel and went to the door. Body language spoke volumes about there being more between them than a simple doctor-nurse relationship. He rolled his eyes at Fyfe, slipped the card into his breast pocket, excused himself, and followed her out leaving the two police officers alone with the accused man.

'Sorry to take you away from your golf,' Sapalski said.

'Probably less grief for me in the long run,' Fyfe answered.

'You weren't playing well then?'

'For me, I was playing well. A couple of shots went straight. Is this our man then?'

'As good as we've got,' Sapalski replied. 'At the locus red-handed, clutching the bloodstained murder weapon.'

'Not a bad prosecution case. Who is he?'

'A blank so far, sir. His fingerprints are being checked but I'm not convinced that will help. It's Sunday so we probably won't get the result until tomorrow.'

'Curious, this,' Fyfe said, lifting one of the unconscious man's arms. 'Look at his hands. Look at the fingernails. They're beautifully manicured, a professional person's hands. He's not from the artisan class. He's not your average housebreaker. He must have been in it for the fun of it.'

Sapalski studied the floppy hand, each finger in turn. 'You're right,' he concluded.

'The first of Zena's little paradoxes.'

'Pardon?'

'Just thinking aloud.'

'Maybe he only did big houses,' Sapalski suggested. 'Antiques and that kind of stuff. Posh side of the business.'

'Maybe,' Fyfe conceded doubtfully. 'But did he really need overalls and a balaclava? Bit of the romantic there. Bit of an adventurer.'

'A romantic adventurer turned savage killer with a meat-tenderising mallet. Not a happy ending.'

'It's believable. The first thing that came to hand. Not every story has the fabled happy ending. What else should I know?'

Sapalski filled Fyfe in on the details of Marianne Dunne finding the body, and big Sandy Ramensky mooching about morosely. When he told him about poor terminally ill Lorna back at the lodge house, he dropped his voice respectfully. He told him about Ramensky's fantasy of transferring the life from a living person into his daughter to save her, and offered it tentatively as a very long-shot as a motive for killing old Zena if they wanted an alternative to the simple option of the killer in the balaclava. Fyfe was not as sceptical as Sapalski seemed to think he should be. Fyfe automatically connected little Lorna with Lorna Doone who was fixed in his mind as a tragic literary heroine although he couldn't remember the author or the ultimate outcome of the storyline. Had Lorna's parents condemned their baby when they named her?

Sapalski's voice went up in volume again to describe Zena McElhose's blameless life and her violent death. There was no evidence of forced entry to the house, raising the possibility that the killer was known to her, or perhaps she had simply forgotten to lock the door. He set out the calculated time scale and said that, again because it was Sunday, the post-mortem wouldn't be done until the next day. Fyfe told Sapalski about Dr McInnes's medical opinion. Everything inevitably came back full circle to John Doe lying on the bed beside them under his watchful electronic guardians.

'Not really much point in looking any further, Inspector Sapalski, is there?' Fyfe said. 'We might as well sit here and wait for our pal to wake up and tell us the whole story. The problem with that is that the public would think we weren't doing enough to earn our salaries.'

'If the fingerprints are negative tomorrow we'll do a mug-shot and hand it out to the media. Somebody somewhere's got to know who he is.'

'Okay. In the meantime, I'd like to see the scene of the crime in old Zena's palace down by the seaside.'

'Of course,' Sapalski said. 'You wouldn't mind if I shot home for a couple of hours, would you, sir? I know I'm in charge of this inquiry and normally I wouldn't ask but my wife's pregnant and I'd just like to check that there's nothing wrong.'

'Check that everything's all right.'

'I'm sorry?'

'Always think positively, John. Don't worry yourself about something being wrong. You are going home to check that everything is all right.'

'You don't mind then?'

'You've done the donkey work for the day. No point in putting in face time if it's not going to be productive. I know how important it is to keep on the right side of the women in our lives. Besides, it's better to ensure life than clear up after death, don't you agree?'

'It was just seeing that poor kid Lorna today and the effect it was having on her parents. It really got through to me.'

'Go home, John.'

'Thanks.'

17

Sunday, 14.37

She had only been in his house once before, a long time ago. She had gone to collect documents when he was laid up with a broken ankle after falling down the office steps. He had answered the door and taken her up to his study, limping so badly on the stairs in his plaster cast that he needed to hold on to her elbow for support. At one point she had thought he was going to put his arm right round her shoulder and she almost fainted at the prospect. But he didn't. It was when his wife was still alive. They made it to the top of the stairs and he could walk more easily on the flat.

The study was a big wood-panelled, book-lined room with a huge leather-topped desk in the centre. He always kept it scrupulously tidy with his word processing screen, keyboard and printer aligned with the edges. He had sat down at the desk and finished annotating the last few pages of a sheaf of papers with the platinum fountain pen the other partners in the law firm had presented him with to mark its twentieth anniversary. She stood deferentially by his shoulder waiting for him.

When the paperwork was complete he lifted his ankle on to the desk and asked her to sign the cast. Then he had insisted she stay for coffee. Joan was away for some reason and she had to help him down the stairs to the kitchen. He chatted away happily, entertaining her with small talk and church gossip. She was her usual icily polite, taciturn self. Only later, once she was away and on her own, did her imagination begin to run wild on what might have been.

Now Maureen Gilliland was back in that study once more, seated in that same chair at that same desk. The desk was, surprisingly, rather untidy with books and folders scattered haphazardly about its surface, and the keyboard disconnected from the screen. She cleared a space on the green leather and

64

sorted it all out. The screen glowed green, blinking at her as if she had just woken it up. She typed in Val's password. She wrote yesterday's date in the top right-hand corner, putting the year first, then the month and then the day in her fantasy lover's personal idiosyncratic style. She typed quickly, the content already composed inside her head, fascinated to see the idea created in front of her eyes.

'I am going to see Zena. This must end,' she wrote. 'I must tell her our affair cannot continue. It was a mistake I now bitterly regret. If she will not accept it she must suffer the consequences. There is no alternative. The truth is I love Maureen. I cannot help myself. I have always loved Maureen. I love her passionately. How could I have been so foolish as to betray her? I will always love her. I hope she will forgive me.'

It seemed so right to see it written down. There was a smile on Gilliland's face as she took a sheet of notepaper with the distinctive Randolph and Runciman heading from a drawer and prepared the letter for printing. She fed the paper into the printer and the inkjet head began to whisper across the page. Val's fountain pen was in another drawer. Its cap was stiff. Twice she tried to pry it off and failed. The third time it came away. She caught sight of her distorted reflection in the narrow rounded surface of the platinum. She looked tiny, insignificant, a million miles away. Her motivating sense of impatience was replaced with calm.

She raised the letter to her mouth and kissed it. 'I forgive you, Val my darling,' she said softly.

She signed the letter with a flourish, recreating the loops and curves of Valentine Randolph's name and customary identifying mark. After all, with his connivance she had regularly forged his signature on a range of documents. No one had ever noticed.

The smile faded quickly while she was admiring her handiwork. She put the pen in her handbag and tidied the desk so that the letter lay exactly in the centre of the green leather rectangle. She looked back at it from the doorway then went downstairs, moving with sudden haste and urgency. Impatience had overwhelmed her. She was glancing over her shoulder as though somebody was chasing her through the empty house. She went through the kitchen where they had shared coffee and into the adjoining garage. The red Mercedes, all washed and waxed, shone brilliantly under the harsh strip lights. Gilliland slipped into the white leather driving seat. She pulled down the sun visor and the ignition keys fell into her waiting hand. The car's engine was so silent she thought at first it had not started but then she saw exhaust fumes ballooning up at the rear. She flicked the electronic remote and the wide up-and-over door began to open. She pushed the gear lever into place and the car jumped forward. Its aerial scraped the bottom of the still-rising door, but she was out and along the driveway and into the street with Valentine's house falling away behind her.

18

Sunday, 16.02
Fyfe liked to work alone, without distractions or interruptions. So he was glad that Sapalski had gone home to hold hands with his pregnant wife and leave him to get on with it. He knew enough of the details and the circumstances of old Zena's murder. At first glance, the facts suggested he would have been better employed staying at Gleneagles for the afternoon round but, as Sir Duncan had pontificated, the most straightforward open and shut case sometimes turned up the most inconvenient lines of inquiry. Zena's fate might yet produce a paradox for him to solve that would defeat the obvious logic of the situation.

He drove across the city in the gathering gloom of early afternoon. The shape of an incoming plane slid across the sky on the horizon, reminding him that Angela would be arriving soon, perhaps on that very plane. And that turned his thoughts to Hilary. She hadn't phoned him back because she didn't know his number, not because she didn't want to speak to him. He decided to try her again, pulling into the side of the road in a street overhung by trees that caused silent shadows to slash and whip across the grey and black atmosphere of the car. The wind had risen considerably. The rain was getting heavier. A big storm was brewing over the city. Fyfe rolled back his sleeve and read the fading number she had written there, although he knew it by heart anyway.

'Hello,' she answered.

'Hilary. This is David from the party last night. Remember?'

'Oh yes. Sorry I was so short with you earlier. I couldn't talk then.'

'No problem.'

'My husband was in the house. In fact he was standing right beside me. I had an attack of confused guilt.'

'Has it subsided yet?'

'Totally. I was hoping you'd phone back, David. I hadn't realised I didn't know your number. You should have written it on my arm.'

'I'd like to do that.'

'I'd like you to do that too.'

Fyfe had a deep sense of foreboding. He shouldn't be doing this. He should walk away from Hilary and keep things simple. But she was a seductive bundle of trouble and he couldn't stop himself. The truth was he didn't want to stop himself. He even viewed her, in some strange way, as an antidote to Angela, both of them appearing to him as they had done in those short black dresses. It was a mystical link, as inexplicable as it was unavoidable. The time was right for the two of them, him and Hilary. It might never be right again if he let this chance pass by. He didn't intend to.

'I thought maybe you'd like to go for a drink tonight?'

'Where?'

'I don't know. Somewhere quiet.'

'It's quiet here.'

'Where? In your home?'

'Yes.'

'What about your other half?'

'He's away on an overnight trip.'

'So you're all alone?'

'Sad, isn't it?'

'I don't like it when people are sad. I've just got a few things to do then I'll probably be free in a couple of hours.'

'I'm waiting. Bring a nice bottle of wine.'

'Red or white?'

'Red. Full-bodied.'

'Anything else?'

'That's about all we need.'

'And you promise you won't be sad any more?'

'I promise if you come and see me.'

'We can pretend we're still at the party.'

'If you like.'

She told him her address and when she had gone Fyfe felt a flush of warmth spread outwards from the base of his neck. Here was another woman to complicate his life. How many times had he been down this road? Would he never learn? There was a touch of guilt too. Sally was waiting for him at home with the dogs. That was where, in a perfect world, he should go, but he knew he wouldn't. Instead he phoned Sally from the shadow-whipped car and said he was stuck on a murder inquiry and might have to spend the night in the city. If Hilary kicked him out when the bottle of wine was finished he would drive home and say he had got finished earlier than anticipated. He liked to keep his options open.

He drove on to Zena's house. There were two uniforms at the gate, and another one sitting on his own in a car beside the big house. He asked for the odd-job man to be sent up in about fifteen minutes and went in past the lodge with its tightly closed curtains all but concealing the lights shining outside.

The officer at the house got out of his car and offered to act as a guide but once he had shown Fyfe down the side path to the rear entrance he was sent back to his lonely sentry post. Beyond the blue and white tape that marked the entrance to the crime scene Fyfe could apply his full concentration to a mental recon-struction of events. One summer long ago, when he was a wet-behind-the-ears beat constable, he had read every Sherlock Holmes story ever written and dreamt of becoming the world's greatest detective. It was far too late now to realise that ambition.

The alarm system was switched off. A winking red light on a control panel like the Starship Enterprise showed that it was on stand-by. Fyfe passed quickly through the utility room and into the kitchen. The place where Zena's body had been found was marked with red sticky tape because the floor was too smooth and shiny to take chalk marks. The kitchen was ordinary, banal, like a million other kitchens in a million other houses. It betrayed no hint of what had happened there. The floor had been scrubbed clean of blood.

Fyfe followed Sapalski's description and went out into the hallway. He saw himself in the huge wall mirror and was momentarily disorientated. Then the interior landscape sorted itself out; the wooden doorways on each side and the pieces of furniture and the elephant's foot stuffed full of umbrellas and walking-sticks. The alcove door was standing open. There was more red tape in a crude body shape on the tiled floor where the mystery man's body had been discovered between the solid front door and the glass-panelled inner door. If there had been any blood, it too had been cleaned up. Fyfe patted the porcelain Dalmatian on the head and waited for psychic intuition to give him an important insight. Nothing happened.

He went into each room, walking round, studying the family pictures in the silver frames. He picked a person in the photographs he presumed to be Zena and followed her visible progress as she developed and matured and finally, upstairs in the main bedroom, grew old.

'Why did you die, Zena?' he asked her. 'What's the paradox here?'

In the first-floor drawing-room with its huge break-front bookcase and mahogany dining-table there was an ornate carriage clock ticking loudly on the black marble mantelpiece of the fireplace. Two Chinese-style dog-lions with green gem-stone eyes sat on either side of it. Fyfe opened the french windows and stepped out on to the balcony that ran three-quarters the length of the front of the house. He leaned on the railing and looked out over the trees to the sea where it filled the wide estuary of the River Forth and the ill-defined land beyond where lights emerged and disappeared in the grey and drifting mist.

'It's called a widow's walk,' Ramensky said behind him. 'A lot of the houses around here have them.'

Fyfe turned, surprised by Ramensky's presence and annoyed that he should have been allowed on to the crime scene by himself. Then he noticed the uniformed policeman hovering in the background and relaxed. He nodded to dismiss him and waved Ramensky out on to the balcony, shifting to one side to accommodate him. The big man had to duck below the lintel. When he straightened up his head reached the rain gutter on the edge of the sloping roof.

'You must be Sandy Ramensky. A Polish name, isn't it?'

The newcomer nodded. 'And you're Chief Inspector Fyfe, the head man.'

'The one that's been around the longest anyway.'

'More questions?'

'We've all got our little empires to protect. If I rely on underlings, what's the point of my existence? What did you say this balcony was called?'

'Captains' wives used to stand out on walks like these and look out for returning ships.'

'How come they're called widow's walks then?'

'Because so many captains and ships never came back.'

'And the wives kept on walking.'

'Exactly, because they could never know for certain what happened to the ships. They kept look-out for years on end sometimes.'

'No radios in those days. No portable phones.'

'No way to know if their men were dead or alive.'

'Mrs McElhose was a widow,' Fyfe said. 'She would have all the proper certification though. Mr McElhose was a banker, I believe.'

'I never knew him. She used to sit out here in the summer, taking tea. She brought out a chair and a table with a white cloth. You could see her from the lodge. Watching her, it could have been the eighteenth century.'

'She was murdered in our century, however. If she had survived it would have been a much quainter crime.

'Would it now?'

'Hamesucken it would have been called, a term unique to Scots law. It means the crime of committing an assault on a person in his or her own dwelling house.'

'Fascinating.'

'Isn't it? But since old Zena succumbed it becomes plain murder, an ugly word with no redeeming quality or romance. Who do you think killed her then?'

Ramensky went a little way along the balcony and stood at the railing, looking outwards. 'I don't know,' he said, shaking his head.

'You've done your statement?'

'Yes. I've put down everything I know. I'm already late for work.'

'Some of my colleagues think you should be a suspect.'

Ramensky's head turned on his massive shoulders. Fyfe regretted raising the subject. The man would easily overpower him in a fight, snap his neck like a used matchstick. He checked that the french windows were open if he had to make a dash for safety. Below them in the driveway the policeman walked over to his car, slid inside and pulled the door shut.

'You know how people's thought processes work,' Fyfe went on. 'We don't have a butler to blame so the odd-job man must have done it. Big men are always the first to be associated with acts of violence.'

'What about the guy inside the front door?'

'An even better suspect but our highly intensive training warns us never to accept a situation at face value. After all, you could have put him there to divert attention.'

'Why would I do that?'

'A diversion.'

'From what?'

'Your guilt.'

'But why would I want to kill Mrs McElhose?'

'So your daughter Lorna will live.'

Ramensky's reaction was slow and deliberate. He gripped the top of the rail, tilted his head back and laughed mirthlessly. Fyfe laughed too. There was a degree of empathy between them. He was safe. Ramensky was no murderer. He was a void of bottomless despair standing there with the sparse rain beginning to fall on his upturned face.

'If only it was so simple,' Ramensky said.

'It's a respectable theory. Dates back to the ancient Greeks and their penchant for regular human sacrifices to pacify the gods. Red Indians believed they acquired the strength of an enemy killed in battle. You're not on any original track really.'

'I would have done it in a minute if it would have helped Lorna.'

'But you didn't?'

'I thought about it,' Ramensky replied seriously. 'I thought about killing myself too. I had this idea I would lie down beside

71

her and cut my wrists and my life force or whatever it is would pass over somehow and she would be miraculously cured and get to grow up. I've thought about it a hundred times. I've studied it. It even has a scientific name. Metempsychosis, the transmigration of human souls into new bodies. But it wouldn't be Lorna then, would it? If only it was so simple.'

'Why wouldn't it work?'

'Because you wouldn't be able to focus the changeover,' Ramensky argued reasonably. 'How could I guarantee that Mrs McElhose's soul, once it was released, would be available for Lorna? Besides, body and soul are separate. It is Lorna's body that is dying. Her soul is strong.'

Fyfe had no answer to such a deceptively rational argument, although he suspected a course in philosophy might provide him with one. He nodded and looked away from Ramensky's entreating stare.

'Why did you call her Lorna?' he asked.

'What?'

'Lorna. Where did the name come from?'

'I don't know. Marianne chose it. What's that got to do with anything?'

'Nothing. I'm just curious about names. How is she? Lorna?'

The explosion of laughter that came from Ramensky made the hairs prickle on the back of Fyfe's neck. He wished he hadn't asked the question. It was stupid. There was no need for it. He knew the answer.

'Another day closer to death. What do you expect?'

Fyfe coughed and tried to cover his embarrassment by ushering Ramensky inside and closing and locking the french windows. They went down through the house, passing the locations of the bodies without comment, and out the back door, raising the blue and white crime scene marking line over their heads to exit. Fyfe checked his watch as he followed Ramensky up the side path. He had some time to spare.

'Is your wife asleep?'

'No,' Ramensky said. 'She can't.'

'Does she know about your theorising?'

'No,' he said too hastily. 'She's made a statement as well.'

'She'll know the answers to give me then.'

They took Fyfe's car the short distance to the lodge, leaving it beside the incident caravan where the policeman on guard now sat pretending not to be reading a book while drinking tea from a polystyrene cup. Fyfe was no sooner inside the door of the lodge than he was affected by an atmosphere of unreality that made him desperate to escape. The central heating was on full, making it oppressively warm. He decided not to ask too many questions. He wanted to get this over with as quickly as possible.

Marianne Dunne came over to him with one hand outstretched and her tragic wide-eyed daughter Lorna astride her hip. Ramensky made the introductions and left to go to work. Fyfe felt the slight pressure of the mother's handshake and the fixed stare of the child.

'She won't sleep,' Marianne explained. 'Too much excitement and comings and goings today. It's too early.'

'How is she?' Fyfe asked before he could stop himself.

'Bearing up.'

Marianne was so small and delicate compared to the lumbering Ramensky. She had a haunted look about her, a vacancy behind the eyes that cancelled out the superficial, tear-dry smile. She was a woman on the verge of insanity. Outwardly she was controlled and assured, yet she was actually inconsolable and unreachable by anyone. The murder of Zena McElhose was an unimportant sideshow compared to what was happening to her daughter. Fyfe imagined she was thinking he should be there to investigate the injustice being done to a child who had been condemned to die so young. Who was the prime suspect in her inevitable death? What was the defence case? There was a genuine paradox to be resolved in Lorna's case. Who was to blame?

No wonder Sapalski had felt the need to go home to restore his grip on reality after having to face this, Fyfe thought. He tried to take hold of Lorna's hand to show his compassion but she snatched it away and hid her face against her mother's neck.

Fyfe asked his questions and Marianne answered them from behind her self-imposed barrier. He did not take any notes. He did not learn anything new. He made his excuses and left, gulping down the cold air outside as if he had just surfaced from deep under water. He looked up at the sky through the waving branches of the trees and was aware of the raw biological power of his own life force surging through him.

19

The identity of the man in hospital after the murder of the old lady remained a mystery, according to the news on the hour in the never-ending Tam Spurious radio programme. Poor Valentine must still be unconscious, Maureen Gilliland speculated. It wasn't clear if the police knew who he was and were refusing to say or if they had no idea to begin with. Perhaps, even now, he was trying to do a deal to protect his anonymity and his reputation. But he had made his bed and taken Zena McElhose under the covers. It was only fair he should lie on it, exposed for what he was. All's fair in love and war.

Gilliland stood inside the phone box in the street outside the police where Valentine Randolph would fail to turn up for work tomorrow. He was never late. Punctuality with him was an obsession, as it was with her. What a shock the others would get when neither appeared. They would be even more surprised when they learned the truth.

She had driven back in the Mercedes to see that her mother was all right. No problems there. Fed and watered and settled down where she could watch television and contentedly nibble digestive biscuits to her heart's content. It would be the morning before she became aware that her dutiful daughter was gone for good.

Gilliland had been into the office too, sitting in his swivel seat to feel the shape moulded by Val's weight over the years. She had swung around in the chair until the whole familiar room dissolved into a disjointed stream of colours. In a drawer she found a card. It had Manet's *Blonde with Bare Breasts* on the front, the kind of painting most people would expect her to strongly disapprove of, but which she secretly coveted. Inside the message page was blank. She took out his fountain pen and wrote: 'For Maureen. Only we will ever know the truth.' Then his name and three kisses. She put the card in its accompanying envelope, writing her own name on that, and replaced it in the drawer.

74

She got up and put on her coat again before locking up. Outside in the phone box, she wore the little portable radio with the headphones she used for the bus journey to and from work and sang gently to herself.

'I think the washing powder is greatly overrated,' a female caller was saying. 'It just doesn't get my whites white.'

'I find that extremely interesting,' Spurious replied in witheringly sarcastic tones. 'It is sad, is it not, that with the world crumbling around our ears the only subject you wish to discuss on national radio is the effectiveness or otherwise of washing powder?'

'What do you mean?'

'Get a life and keep me out of it. Next caller, please.'

'Hi, Tam. I'm opposed to these building regulations that mean I can't replace my windows without some dickhead from the council coming round and telling me he approves.'

'Really. Would you be happy if your neighbour installed tartan window frames?'

'Well, no.'

'Or if another neighbour decided he liked flashing neon tubes round his panes of glass?'

'No, but – '

'In other words you think everybody should be subject to regulations but your good self.'

'Aye, but there's nothing wrong with my windows.'

'There is however something wrong with your logic.'

'What do you mean?'

'Everybody's wrong but you. Don't you realise laws are made to be impartial and objective and not to favour one person against the other? Everybody or nobody has to conform. It's not a matter of personal choice.'

'Aye, but my windows are fine.'

'Goodbye. Is there no one out there with the intellectual rigour to sustain an argument beyond its initial premise? We homespun philosophers are such lonely people. Ah, another call. Maybe this will be a good one.'

'Tam, do you know what happened when I walked into a bar the other night?'

'No. What happened?'

'I was knocked out.'

'Were you now? Why was that?'

'It was an iron bar.'

Spurious sighed over the sound of manic cackling. The programme dissolved into a run of advertisements. In the phone box Gilliland smiled at the joke, picked up the receiver and pressed a pound coin into the slot. She dialled the programme's number from memory. The call was answered immediately.

'May I speak with Mr Spurious?'

'Okey dokey, darling,' a voice said. 'If you just hang on you're next in the queue.'

She waited patiently. A couple of minutes passed. She put in another pound coin. On the radio the advertisements ended and a furious argument developed between Spurious and a caller with a high-pitched voice over the need for religious education in schools.

'If I had my way I'd ban the bible and replace it with the Kama Sutra. At least the stories in it are enjoyable and much more believable. Some of them anyway.'

'You are a blasphemous sinner,' the caller spluttered.

'Get away. And here's me thinking I was a homo sapiens. Is there anybody else out there? Who's next?'

Gilliland realised it was her. 'See if you can make the bastard's teeth rattle,' she was told. 'You're on air now.'

It was strange hearing Tam Spurious speak in her ear at the same time as she heard him on the radio. She removed one headphone to be able to hear him better and found herself blinking rapidly.

'Yes, caller, what have you got to say for yourself?'

'This murder last night.'

'The old lady?'

'Yes.'

'What about it?'

'The man they found there. The police don't know who he is.'

'Is that so? Do you?'

'Yes.'

'Go on, tell us then.'

'His name is Valentine Randolph, senior partner in a law firm in the city.'

The sudden loud blast of rock music from the radio disorientated her, making her jerk her head to the side. She hadn't heard Val's name repeated. They had blanked it out.

'How do you know this?' Spurious was asking.

'I know.'

'Who are you?'

She didn't reply.

'Why should I believe you?'

'Look for his car.' She recited the registration number. 'When you find it you'll understand.'

'Where is this car?'

She hung up, pulled off the remaining headphones and walked away from the phone box. One way or the other everybody would know about Val soon enough. And then they would know about her too. She hummed quietly to herself as she slid behind the wheel of the red Mercedes. The seat fitted perfectly round her. It was warm and comfortable. She imagined her fantasy lover was in the passenger seat beside her, leaning over, grabbing her knee, running his hand up the inside of her leg, kissing her neck. She put her head back and moaned with the frightening intensity of her unreal, unrequited passion.

'Maureen? Is that you?'

She froze. Her eyes snapped open. Gregor Runciman's face was framed in the V-shaped space at the top of the open car door. He was leaning down, preventing her from closing the door. He looked puzzled; more than that, shocked. His eyes were dangerously pink, like an albino rabbit's, surrounded by a flat whiteness of pale flesh. His lips moved and she heard the words but could not answer them. She told herself to be calm but panic paralysed her and squeezed at her insides. She felt the warm dampness between her legs and realised she had wet herself again.

'Maureen, what are you doing here?' Runciman asked. 'Have you been in the office?'

He was pulling at the door but she held it tight, aware of the pain it was causing in the muscle of her right arm. Had he seen her in the phone box? Did he know what she was doing? Had he been watching her in the office? Why was he here? Was he following her? Had she been found out already? She had to get away from him.

77

'Just hold on a minute, Maureen,' Runciman said, and there was an edge to his voice that frightened her. 'Wait there. I'll get in the other side. I have to speak to you. It's important.'

The car door slammed shut, hurting Gilliland's wrist. Runciman was moving round the front of the car, hand resting on the wing as he stepped off the kerb. Gilliland seized her chance. She switched on the ignition, rammed the gearstick into first gear, released the clutch and stamped on the accelerator. The Mercedes leapt forward. Runciman, his face rigid with shock and surprise, was lifted off his feet. He rolled on to the bonnet. His knees struck the windscreen, then his hands and he was pushed to one side, falling away. Gilliland, smiling vacantly at her own reflection, moved her head to be able to see him in the rear-view mirror, crawling on all fours on the ground far behind.

20

Sunday, 16.10
John Sapalski got what Wilma asked for, macaroni with jam doughnuts on the side washed down by a cherry-flavoured fizzy drink that gave her the most terrible wind. She was sitting, hugely pregnant, in the living-room with her feet up on a cushion-covered chair and all the necessities within easy reach. She read one of a supply of books and watched the television at the same time and when she got bored she played with one of those children's games where you have to roll tiny steel balls into holes on the horizontal base by tilting it from side to side.

He hung about but she didn't seem too bothered whether he was there or not. He knelt down beside her and put his ear against the mound of her stomach to listen to all the whooshing and gurgling noises that so fascinated him. Wilma patted him on the head.

'I'm fine,' she said. 'Don't worry about me. It's not an illness, you know. Having a baby is a wholly natural event.'

'Even our baby?'

'Yes, even our baby. It won't be the first to come into this world, believe it or not. Might not even be the last.'

Sapalski ran the palms of his hands over her stomach. They had been to natural childbirth classes at his insistence to learn breathing and pain relief techniques. Wilma had agreed but reserved the right to be pumped full of drugs so that she wouldn't feel anything at all when it came to the crucial moment. How could he argue? He had done his bit. Everything was up to her now. The division of labour was quite clear.

'Go back to work, John,' she said.

'I don't like leaving you on your own.'

'I won't be on my own,' she replied, cradling her stomach. 'I've got our baby to keep me company.'

'I should go back.'

'Back you go then.'

Sapalski stood up. Wilma didn't know about the murder of Zena McElhose. He didn't want to upset her by describing the terrible fate of a lonely old woman. Wilma thought it was just another routine investigation he was in charge of. He hadn't told her about Fyfe being shunted in above him to supervise. He hadn't told her about his encounter with little Lorna and her terminal illness. He hadn't explained his overpowering urge to rush home to be with her. He hadn't conveyed the substance of his fears and worries. All he had done was make her macaroni and jam doughnuts and annoy her by fussing around uselessly.

His feelings of anxiety were passing now that he had established Wilma was safe, or at least as safe as he knew. There were no guarantees that the biological formation of his offspring was progressing without mishap inside her womb. A fatal genetic flaw might be insinuating itself as he stood there looking down. That wasn't something he could protect her against.

'For goodness sake, John, will you stop it. You're making me nervous.'

'Sorry. I'll leave you to it then.'

'I won't wait up.'

'I don't know when I'll be back.'

'Any emergencies or early starts and you can be sure I'll have every policeman in the force hunting you down. You won't miss any of the blood and gore. That's a promise.'

He bent down and kissed her on the forehead. 'I'll leave then.'

'If you say it often enough you just might.'

Sapalski backed out of the room and picked up his coat from

the floor in the hall where he had flung it on his way in. He decided to phone before he left to find out if there were any developments in the case. He couldn't think of any there might be unless their mystery man woke up at the hospital. He got through to Graham Evans who had been delegated to headquarters to begin setting up a computer database with the first rush of statements from the door-to-doors.

'What's the score?' he asked.

'Possible line on John Doe,' Evans replied. 'A woman phoned the local radio station and gave a name.'

'Who?'

'Valentine Randolph. A New Town lawyer and businessman. Senior partner in Randolph and Runciman, a blue chip firm. Luckily we had a car passing his address. No one home. Could be a wind-up. We're trying to find him.'

'Who was the woman?'

'Anonymous call to the Tam Spurious show.'

'How genuine, do you reckon?'

'Difficult to say. She did give the number of a car that is registered in Randolph's name. The caller seemed to think it was significant information but the garage at his house is empty.'

'Have you checked the streets round old Zena's house?'

'No.'

'If she's genuine that will be what she means and you'll find it there. If he drove there he didn't get the chance to drive away again, did he?'

'I never thought of that.'

'And does the radio station have a record of where the call came in from?'

'I'll check.'

Sapalski paused, thinking whether there was anything else he could set in motion to find out if this was a breakthrough or a blind alley. He would have known already if he had stayed on. But the prospect was exciting. Wealthy New Town lawyers didn't normally walk around in overalls, balaclavas, and surgical gloves. He remembered the neatly manicured fingernails. If it was true, there was an extremely strange story to flesh out in the reconstruction of Zena's last hours on earth.

'Find the partners in his law firm too. Maybe they know where this chap Randolph is.'

'We're on to that. By the way, so are the newspapers. I think Tam Spurious called them before he called us. They will be queuing up outside Randolph's as I speak.'

'It's done now. We'll have to live with it. Where is Chief Inspector Fyfe?'

'Vanished. Should I contact him?'

'No. Let's wait and see if this stands up before dragging him in. We've already ruined one round of golf for him this afternoon, let's not ruin his entire day.'

21

Sunday, 16.22

Fyfe found an off-licence that was just closing and persuaded the shopkeeper to give him enough time to buy a bottle of wine. He grabbed the first one he came to on the shelves, a Sicilian red, without looking at the price and had to pay a lot more than he expected to, scraping together just enough loose change to cover the cost.

He sat in his car opposite Hilary's address for several minutes, watching and waiting. It was a first-floor flat on the end of a terraced row marked off by a succession of walls and hedges. Its entrance was at the side through a gate and down the side of a garage. The light was on in her flat and the one directly below. Seagulls perched among the chimney pots. A smirr of rain was falling. The street was full of cars but empty of people, except for occasional pedestrians hurrying past followed by the vapour trails of their breath. The surface of the road shone wetly. He phoned in to headquarters and deliberately didn't say where he was or what he was doing. Sapalski wasn't back from his visit home, but once he was he could handle any routine stuff that cropped up. Fyfe was too senior an officer for anybody there to demand an explanation. He eventually found Detective Sergeant Bill Matthewson who was on the fringe of the investigation and didn't really know what was going on. The golf party had yet to return from Gleneagles so at least they had got their priorities right and there couldn't be anything too dramatic under way. A cryptic message had come in for Fyfe from one of his better criminal contacts, Donaldson MacDuff, but it didn't seem to be desperately urgent. He had sounded drunk and said he would call back the next day. Matthewson quickly ran out of things to pass on.

Fyfe's curiosity was not stirred. He knew he should go back but he had more pressing business he didn't want to ignore. He decided to let Sapalski and his team get on with it and wait for developments. He could afford half an hour of rest and relaxation before plunging into the fray again. That kind of time period was easily explained away, if an accounting ever became necessary. He made a conscious effort to put Zena McElhose and everything associated with her to the back of his mind. Hilary appeared at the front of it in her short black dress leaning casually with her back against the wall inside the circle of his arm.

Fyfe crossed to Hilary's door. A security light switched on automatically when he was half-way along the path, briefly dazzling him. He rang the bell and heard its muted buzz, then the sounds of movement and footsteps rumbling downstairs. The door opened and Hilary stood in front of him wearing a pair of faded blue jeans and a plain white T-shirt. He could see she wasn't wearing a bra. Her feet were bare. Pale eyeshadow and lipstick. Pink cheeks. Flurry, blown-dry hair. Wonderful welcoming smile. Gold chains jumbled at her throat. Fyfe wondered if he should kiss her in greeting, but before he could decide she had stepped forward, placed her hands on his shoulders and bobbed up to kiss him on the cheek.

'It's you then,' she said. 'I'm glad.'

'Sorry I took so long but I was delayed.'

'Crime-fighting out there?'

'Somebody's got to do it.'

'Are you coming in?'

'For a little while. I'm actually on duty.'

'Come on in anyway.'

'Is it safe?'

'As safe as you like.'

'How safe is that? Here's the wine.'

She took it by the neck and read the label. 'Very nice,' she decided. 'You do have good taste.'

'Thanks for the compliment.'

He followed her and the subtle trail of perfume up the internal stairs. One of the back pockets of her jeans was torn and hanging off. She walked on the balls of her feet, moving with an athletic bounce. On the landing she helped Fyfe off with his coat and motioned him to go into the sitting-room. It was simply furnished with two sofas and a deep armchair. The curtains were drawn. Light came from a pair of floor-level lamps beside the fireplace which had a tall arched mirror above it and a deerskin rug in front. A low glass-topped coffee table with books and magazines blocked the main window, and a furniture unit with ornaments and stuff on back-lit shelves was against the back wall. A rubber plant grew out of a copper bucket, reaching up and bowing under the ceiling. Other plants were dotted all around. Music was playing. A female vocalist crooned like a high-pitched Bing Crosby. Fyfe didn't recognise her voice. He took off his jacket and laid it across the arm of a sofa. He was loosening his tie when Hilary came back into the room with the wine bottle and two glasses, kicking the door shut with her heel.

'Sit down,' she said. 'Don't be shy.'

Fyfe sat on the sofa, sinking into it too far for comfort and having to wriggle forward to balance on the edge. Hilary sat cross-legged on the floor a yard from him. She filled the glasses, making a great fuss about ensuring there was exactly the same amount in both. When she was satisfied she handed one to Fyfe.

'Cheers,' they said simultaneously, maintaining eye contact over the crystal clink of the touching glasses and the first drink of wine.

'Well, Chief Inspector Fyfe, I didn't think you'd come tonight.'

'Why not?'

She made a face. 'I just didn't, not after I'd given you such short shrift when you called earlier.'

'It would take more than that to deter me.'

'Neil was beside me. I should have played it cool but I couldn't think quickly enough on my feet. It's a failing of mine.'

'I often have that problem too.'

'It was easier just to hang up.'

'Who did you say I was?'

'A squash partner looking for a game.'

'That was quick thinking. You must have done it before.'

'No. Only with squash partners. You're unique. I haven't

invited anybody back home since I was a carefree teenager in pig-tails and bobby sox.'

'You don't make a habit of picking up men at parties then?'

'No.' She was deadly serious.

'Why me then?'

'I liked the look of you.'

'Flattery will get you everywhere. I liked the look of you too. Wait till I get my tenses right. I like the look of you now.'

She did look extremely attractive kneeling in front of him. He wanted to reach out and stroke her hair, then run his hand down her neck and down to where the T-shirt fell vertically from the horizontal line formed by the peaks of her small breasts. The nipples were just discernible through the material if he looked closely enough. Her hips and legs strained against the shrink-wrap jeans. Fyfe remembered back to Angela and how she flaunted her body for him the night he discovered her among the debris and the dead bodies in a place, he now realised, that was only a few miles from where he was now. A night of unrestrained lust with the lady in black in return for a future of guilt and vulnerability with his haul of stolen money stashed away. Why had he done it? How could he have been so stupid? And now what did Angela want with him after so long? She was going to blackmail him in some form or another. And he would have no choice but to obey her. It was called consequences, a game he had played as a child.

'I'm a married woman,' Hilary said. 'Fifteen years the virtuous wife.'

'And I'm a married man. Something else we have in common.'

'I'm not going to sleep with you tonight.'

He shrugged. 'Pity. That takes all the suspense out of the evening.'

'I didn't want you to get the wrong idea. I must have misled you last night at the party but I was a wee bit drunk. Then there was your phone call today and me inviting you round here. You must have thought I was desperate.'

'I said the suspense had gone out of the evening, not the enjoyment.'

'You're not angry then?'

'Disappointed would be a better word.'

'Oh, you're disappointed with me.'

'Only because I'm a slave to the male stereotype and have a duty to try to sleep with you at the very first opportunity. However, when I step outside the stereotype I'm actually rather pleased.'

'You are?'

'Yes.'

'How am I meant to take that?'

'Like a lady. The pressure's off. I don't have to perform. I only have to be good company, and I can't stay anyway because I'm on duty and supposed to be working.'

'You're not just saying that, are you?'

'Of course not.'

'Good.'

'We're just getting to know each other.'

'Have some more wine.'

Fyfe put his glass on the floor to be filled and slid off the sofa until he was sitting on the floor beside it. His back was propped up and his knees were almost touching Hilary's. She put down the bottle and held a full glass in each hand.

'You know something?' Fyfe said.

'What?'

'There is one thing I'd like to do.'

'What's that?'

'This.'

He put his hand out to touch her chin, then leaned forward. She opened her arms wide so that he wouldn't spill the wine and tilted her head back to make it easier for him. He kissed her lightly on the mouth, allowing the contact to linger, feeling the delicate trace of the tip of her tongue along his upper lip.

'You shouldn't have done that,' she said when he had sat back.

'I've done lots of things I shouldn't have done.'

'And have you regretted them?'

'Mostly.'

'Do you think you'll regret that one?'

'Not yet.'

'Later?'

'Maybe. Who knows?' Fyfe took a glass from her and clinked it against her own. The wine came within a millimetre of spilling.

'Here's to being friends,' he said.

22

Sunday, 16.59

The reporters got to Randolph's house before Sapalski. They were poking about the empty garage, straggling up the driveway and hanging about the gate, having failed to get any response to their ringing of the doorbell. Sapalski was delayed by having to find a Justice of the Peace to sign a search warrant. Strictly speaking, the police might have had a good case if he had decided to kick the door down without official consent but a good lawyer could easily make it look intimadatory and reckless. Sapalski liked to do things by the book, especially when they were accusing a high-flying lawyer or being seriously concerned for his safety, depending on how it panned out. So a JP was found and although he raised a questioning eyebrow when he saw the name and address he signed on the dotted line. The piece of paper in Sapalski's pocket made him feel a lot better when, with the press herded back to a safe distance, a locksmith fumbled around and opened the door. The burglar alarm started to blare.

Once an initial sweep had established there was no one at home, search teams began going through the rooms systematically. Sapalski waited impatiently in the main ground-floor living-room that was cluttered with high quality furniture and obviously expensive antiques. Wealth and affluence oozed from the gilt picture frames and the polished silver in the cabinets under the sculpted plaster of the ceiling. The hee-hawing alarm gave him a sore head and he was extremely grateful when Graham Evans, who had collected the appropriate switch-off key from the neighbours, finally found the command console under the hall stairs and was able to stop the deafening racket.

Everything was coming together neatly, Sapalski thought, and he couldn't understand why he was so nervous. He rubbed his sticky palms together and cadged a cigarette from Evans, although he hadn't smoked since Wilma had announced she was pregnant.

'You sure about this, sir?' Evans said, tapping a cigarette from his packet to hand over.

'I'm sure,' Sapalski answered.

'Here you go then. Enjoy it.'

'One won't kill me.'

'No. Something else will get you before the fags.'

Sapalski sucked the smoke deep into his lungs. His body welcomed the nicotine like a long-lost friend and he immediately felt the craving for more. It took away his headache and steadied the slight tremor he had noticed in his hand when he was making food for Wilma. But it didn't cure his unaccountable nervousness. What was wrong with him? There were names being filled in, motives uncovered, and loose ends tied up. The investigation had all the hallmarks of being a job well done. Case closed almost before the body was cold. Soon he would be able to go home and stay with Wilma. Soon he would be a father, a giver of new life. He decided it must be that prospect that was making him so nervous. Where the hell was Fyfe? It would be good to have him to lean on.

'Nice place,' Evans was saying. 'Must be a rich bastard to live here.'

Sapalski compared his surroundings with the simple decoration and furnishing of his own house, a newly built two-bedroomed semi-detached on an estate of virtually identical semi-detacheds. His entire floor space would have fitted into this one room. He flicked ash over the elaborate brass-edged fireguard into a grate of unburned logs and threw the glowing fag end after it. Evans was going round lifting ornaments and inspecting them the way Sapalski's mother-in-law did when she came to visit.

'Count your blessings,' Sapalski said. 'We might not be able to afford a place like this but we're not lying in hospital about to be charged with murder.'

'Good point,' Evans said. 'Are we sure it's him?'

'Take a look at his photograph.'

There was a definite resemblance in the photograph on top of the bureau to the man in the hospital bed. Evans peered closely and nodded in assent.

'Have you got another cigarette?' Sapalski demanded.

'Sure.'

Before Evans could hand over the cigarette they were called upstairs to what was clearly Randolph's study. A young detective opened a cupboard door that blended in so well with the panelling in the room it had to be pointed out to be noticeable. Inside were four shelves. The bottom two were empty. The others had on them a curious variety of small objects, each widely spaced and sitting on a piece of paper with a cryptic message printed on it in letters and figures. The objects in themselves were fairly unremarkable. It was the neatly ordered way they were displayed that seemed out of the ordinary. There was a squat, half-empty jar of Quink, a miniature of ten-year-old Laphroaig whisky in its round box, a set of car keys with an ancient leather tab, a cat's flea collar, a bookend in the shape of a parrot, a paperweight with integral flower, a crude porcelain bowl, a tin opener, an old street map of Berlin with the city still divided into east and west, a Collins Gem French-English dictionary, a computer disc, and a drinking mug that said it was a present from the Oktoberfest in Munich.

'What's all this about?' Sapalski said out loud. 'This is a pretty strange collection of junk. What does it mean?'

'Maybe it's some kind of Masonic ritual,' Evans said. 'Or a hoard of personal treasures, sentimental value only?'

Sapalski frowned uncertainly. He reckoned the numbers on the pieces of paper were dates although the normal written style was reversed with the month ahead of the day. The dates stretched back a year and formed a clear pattern of monthly intervals. The letters might be people's initials with another element indicating place. People, place, and time. Personal mementoes of meetings, special occasions, special events? He stared at the objects and felt a curious disaffection as if they were relaying some kind of cryptic warning to him. What the hell did it all mean?

A tap on the shoulder by the same young detective who had showed Sapalski the cupboard brought his attention over to the desk in the centre of the room. It too looked unremarkable until he was shown the letter. He bent down and read the neatly printed words, unaware that his lips were moving as he scanned the few sentences. A smile had spread over his face by the time he reached the hand written signature at the end.

'This I can understand,' he said. 'Now we're beginning to have some light shed on it all.'

Evans read the letter in turn and handed Sapalski another cigarette. 'The odds are our anonymous tip-off came from this Maureen. Randolph's aggrieved lover. She's obviously not a happy woman.'

Evans thumbed through his notebook. 'Randolph's personal assistant is a Maureen Gilliland,' he announced.

'Really? I have a feeling we'll be hearing more from Maureen.' He inhaled the calming smoke and relished the prospect of telling Fyfe what they had discovered once he reappeared. 'From the tone of this letter I doubt if she's finished yet.'

23

Sunday, 17.30

Sandy Ramensky should have been at work but instead he was sitting on a high stool at a bar where, like chess pieces on a board, the beer taps stood like pawns in front of the ranks of spirit bottles behind. He had drunk too much beer in the four pubs he had visited one after the other in rapid succession that afternoon. It lay heavily in his stomach, congealed into an indigestible lump that was only slowly being eroded away. He had progressed from beer to vodka, and then dark rum although he didn't like the taste. It was rum that was in the glass he held cradled between his big hands. He would finish the sickly sweet rum but he had had enough of it. He would try whisky next.

Ramensky had left home with the intention of going to work as normal, but had been diverted. The turmoil in his head would give him no peace. A farewell kiss from his dying daughter was like a stiletto blade viciously stabbing him. His crazy theory about life force being passed from the dead to the living had finally been discredited. How did he know? Old Zena McElhose lay dead, and his daughter Lorna's condition had suddenly got worse. So much for divine intervention and the science of metempsychosis. Lorna was too weak now to get out of her bed, reducing Marianne to tears. And all he could do was clench his jaw and open and close his fists and offer to fight the invisible enemy. And the smart cop called Fyfe could see inside his brain, could see the illicit thoughts corralled there surrounded by a fragile fence that could so easily be broken down. Or maybe it was already broken down. Maybe he had killed old Zena and then somehow blacked it out. The bastard Fyfe seemed to know exactly what he was thinking.

Ramensky hadn't lost himself in drink for ages but here he was stumbling into the familiar alcohol-induced fog, killing off another few thousand brain cells so that he didn't have to think about what was happening to him. It was a deceptively simple solution, ruined by the simple fact that he inevitably woke up the next day and had to face it all over again. So he had gone on the wagon, drying out, trying to be strong and terrifying himself with the discovery that he was hopelessly weak.

Now he was losing it once more. The mental fog was narrowing his field of vision. He held on to the glass clutched in his hands, believing it was all that stopped him falling off the stool.

'What is it then?'

He must have called the barmaid over to him. He lifted his head and was taken on his own personal fairground waltzer ride. She stood in front of him, chewing gum, hands on her hips, twitching in time to the music that was an oceanic roar in his ear. She was wearing a flowery shirt and baggy jeans, looking dowdy like the pub she worked in. She had a weary, seen-it-all expression on her face; too long on her feet, too many drunks, too many propositions, too many other people's problems which didn't interest or concern her.

'A Tina Turner,' he muttered.

'What? I can't hear.'

'Tina Turner. Whisky.'

She leaned against the counter, frowned and pursed her lips. There was a tattoo of a purple rose on her upper arm.

'A Tina Turner,' Ramensky repeated.

'What's that?'

'Whisky.'

'What?'

'Black Bush whisky. Tina Turner. On the shelf there.'

He grinned at his own cleverness. The barmaid's face twisted into an expression of affected disgust. She tried to snarl to show her teeth but it ended as an amused smile. She turned and found the Black Bush bottle to pour the drink. Ramensky sat up and downed the dregs of the rum but the action in tilting his head made him lose his balance. He toppled backwards and landed on the floor. Suddenly there were a dozen faces looking down on him, and hands touching him all over, helping him to his feet. He watched with fascination as a hand slipped inside his jacket, fingers seeking the pocket where his wallet was. He grabbed the wrist and pulled it away as he regained his full height. He was holding a skinny, unshaven guy with a hook-nosed profile and a shabby suit. He couldn't have looked more like a pickpocket if he had deliberately dressed for the part. Ramensky raised his arm, still holding the thin wrist, and the man's feet left the floor. He wriggled and hissed like an angry snake.

'Leave him alone,' somebody shouted. 'He didn't do nothing.'

Ramensky was punched in the stomach by a darting shape that ran right on past. It didn't hurt much. Somebody else jumped on his back. He swung round. The pickpocket swung with him, his legs knocking over tables and chairs. Ramensky let go of his wrist and he flew against the wall, crashing straight into it like a cartoon character and falling on to his back. Ramensky reached over his shoulder and got a handful of hair. He heaved a red-haired youngster in a faded Hibs strip over in a high arc and slammed him down on the bar. Somebody kicked Ramensky in the leg, somebody else came rushing at him head down. Ramensky lashed out, making satisfying contact with a soft belly and a hard jaw. His attackers collapsed loudly among the scattered furniture, moaning. Everybody else in the pub had drawn back against the wall as if silently waiting for a sign before moving again. Ramensky swayed where he stood, fists curled into tight balls, gradually feeling the anaesthetic of the outburst of raw violence wear off. Van Morrison kept singing 'Into the Mystic', a special tune he recognised from a time long before Lorna was conceived. Tears of self-pity began to prick at his eyes.

He saw that the barmaid was on the phone, probably calling the police, and he knew he had to get away. He tried to walk to the bar but tripped up and fell against it. He took hold of the boy lying there by the trouser belt, jerked him into a sitting position and then roughly down on to the floor. The bar top had been cleared of glasses. Ramensky tried to snatch the bottle of Black Bush whisky but couldn't reach it. The barmaid shrank into a corner when he climbed on to the bar to extend his reach and managed to grab the bottle by the neck. With as much dignity as he could muster, he returned to the public side of the bar and staggered towards the exit. Van Morrison sang:

I want to rock your gypsy soul
Just like way back in the days of old
And together we will float into the mystic
Come on girl

24

Sunday, 17.45
Time passed quickly. Fyfe found himself sitting in the corner of the sofa with Hilary stretched out along the length of it, her legs partly folded and her head on his upper arm. The hem of the white T-shirt had bunched up round her midriff showing a narrow band of bare flesh where her waist turned into the curve of her hip. Her weight was a pleasant burden he could easily bear, enjoying the feel of her body against his. The deep bass rhythm of the whispering music combined with the heat in the room had a soporific effect. Fyfe could quite happily have gone to sleep there and then with Hilary lying next to him. She had said she wasn't going to sleep with him but it might come to that yet, whether she approved or not. Hilary had her glass balanced on the palm of one hand while she ran the finger and thumb of the other up and down the stem. They were down to the dregs of a second bottle of wine Hilary had produced. His half-hour was up long ago.

She had asked him for police stories and he had recited the tale of the father of a terminally ill child thinking that he could gain some extra time for it by sacrificing the life of another person. No names or places. It was purely theory as he set it out, but he had still told her more than he ever told his own wife

Sally – ex-wife actually, as he was obliged to explain once they were on the subject. But Sally was his partner again after a reconciliation. He regarded himself as married to her.

'Is that why you're here with me?' Hilary had asked with mock sincerity. He had no answer to that particular paradox.

'And what happened to him?'

'Who?'

'The father of the child.'

'Imprisoned for life.'

'What a shame.'

'The law has little or no compassion in such cases.'

Hilary looked up at him momentarily, as if checking he was still there, and then down again. 'Would you be shocked if I asked you something?' she said.

'I doubt it.'

'It's not real, you understand. I would never do it. It's just something I wonder about.'

'What is it?'

'You must meet all sorts of people in your job.'

'A sweetie jar full of them.'

'Is there such a thing out there as a hit man?'

'A hit man? You mean a professional assassin?'

'Yes. I read about them in the papers all the time. Do they exist?'

'Most certainly.'

'You're not just saying that?'

'No. There are people around who will do anything for money.'

'Here? In this city?'

'In any city if you know where to go.'

'They're not in Yellow Pages then?'

'Possibly. Try K for killers, just before Kwikfit tyres and exhausts and after key cutters.'

'How much would it cost?' she asked, glancing up again and causing a ripple of pleasure to run over Fyfe by the movement of her head against his arm.

'Depends,' he said. 'Probably the same price as a couple of double-glazed windows. You're not thinking of having that absent husband of yours bumped off, are you?'

'And live happily ever after? It sounds like a bargain. He is well insured, after all, and he is a bit of a luxury these days. Maybe I should cash him in.'

No alarm bells rang for Fyfe. He had started the conversation off on this tack. He raised his arm to put round her and her head fell against his chest. She cuddled in close. She wasn't serious. He might have only known her for a few hours in total but he believed he knew her well and she wasn't about to ask him to arrange for her husband to be disposed of, professionally or otherwise. She was just day dreaming.

They lay together silently for a few more minutes. The wine was finished. Fyfe could feel the warmth of Hilary's breathing reaching his skin through the thin shirt. He thought she must have fallen asleep when he was suddenly wide awake. He wanted to go but couldn't rouse himself to make the move. Hilary had started him thinking about Ramensky and his blunt denial that he was old Zena's murderer. Suppose he wasn't directly responsible but had hired somebody else to do it on his behalf. Suppose the bloke in the balaclava had been deliberately framed, carted in already unconscious and laid out in the most compromising of positions. Suppose Ramensky wasn't as dumb and slow-witted as he made out. It was far from impossible. Fyfe had unravelled murder plots that had more convoluted lineages.

Fyfe's mind was wandering rapidly now, twisting and turning as it ranged over subjects as various as the meaning of life, a suitable excuse to end his encounter with Hilary, what might have happened if he hadn't abandoned his second round at Gleneagles, a wonder drug discovered in the nick of time to save Sandy Ramensky's daughter, the forgotten name of the author of Lorna Doone, the shape of Hilary's rounded breasts that were within a few inches of his hanging fingers, and tomorrow's lunch with the returning native Angela and whatever grief she had in store for him.

He remembered how he and Angela had lain in bed together just as he was lying with Hilary, her head on his chest, while he regretted what had happened between them. If it was to be blackmail, he decided, he might do worse than consider hiring his own personal hit man to get rid of Angela. Donaldson MacDuff, well-known low-life sauna parlour owner, was rumoured to be branching out into the business on a strictly inter-criminal basis. He might be the answer to Hilary's prayers as well. No evidence against him worth a damn, naturally, just a stack of overdose victims who had developed a taste for lethal cocktails of drugs. But a businessman was always looking for new markets and MacDuff did owe Fyfe a favour for the time he quietly overlooked a bag full of cocaine in a Soft and Gentle sauna cubicle. Favours are granted to be called in at a later date. Maybe he could get cheap rates. In fact one of the messages back at headquarters had been from Duffy, the codename he and MacDuff used for clandestine communication between the civilised and the criminal world. Well, it made life more interesting when it was turned into a game. What did Duffy have to tell him?

Hilary stirred, burrowing in even closer, putting her arm across Fyfe and clutching his free forearm. There was a damp patch on his shirt where she had been breathing. He moved his right arm down until he was holding the side of her rib cage, feeling the solidity of the bones under his hand. She made a contented murmuring sound he took for approval. He wondered what time it was but didn't care. The shrill double burr that came after it was much less welcome.

'Is that a portable phone in your pocket or are you no longer pleased to see me?' Hilary said, rising up.

'I should have turned it off.'

'Too late now. The spell is broken.'

'I don't have to answer it.'

'Yes, you do.'

She climbed to her feet but he grabbed hold of her hand so that she couldn't fully straighten up. Her face was level with his, her hair in disarray. She offered no resistance when he kissed her and once again he felt the tip of her tongue slide over his top lip and teeth. The shrill burring continued. It was Hilary who eventually broke the contact of their mouths.

'I don't have to answer it,' he repeated.

Hilary retrieved the phone from his jacket on the floor and handed it to him. 'Yes, you do,' she said on her way out of the room.

Fyfe sighed and submitted, reasoning that here was the excuse he needed to be able to leave Hilary with honour. Hopefully, he could come back for more since he had behaved himself. He turned his attention to the phone, guessing that it would be

Sapalski, unpleasantly surprised when it was the Chief Constable Sir Duncan Morrison who spoke.

'Where are you, David? I've just found out.'

'I'm just touring the back of the McElhose property,' he lied. 'I was looking for means of easy entry. How was the golf?'

'Best forgotten. We're just leaving Gleneagles now. It's a bit embarrassing, this guy Randolph, isn't it?'

Fyfe didn't know what the chief was talking about. Who was Randolph? He was going to have to think on his feet, and think fast if he wasn't going to fall flat on his face. In the past he had carried his resignation letter around with him all the time. It lacked only a date to make it authentic. The plan was to slap it in when the mood moved him because he was independently wealthy thanks to his clandestine deal with Angela. But, after a while, he had torn it up, worried that resignation might be forced on him if he was knocked unconscious in an accident and the letter was found on him. It was the same kind of reasoning used by his mother when she made him put on clean underwear, warning that without it he would be shown up if he was involved in an accident and was taken to hospital. If it became necessary he could just cut the call off, claim atmospheric interference, and find out what was going on before making contact again.

'Why should it be embarrassing, sir?' he asked carefully.

'I know him. Val Randolph's been a dinner guest in my house a couple of times, for God's sake. Not so long ago either. He was a charming bugger, I seem to remember, though it's his partner Gregor Runciman I know socially.'

Val Randolph must be the man in the balaclava, Fyfe was thinking. He must have regained consciousness or they must have identified him some other way, fingerprints perhaps. Sapalski should have come to Fyfe immediately with the information but the bastard had probably decided to run the show himself and make no effort to bring him in. Fyfe couldn't blame him. He should have been concentrating on the murder investigation rather than Hilary's bone structure. Never mind, the situation was not beyond rescue as long as he played it cool. Who the fuck was this bloke Randolph? How come he went to dinner parties with the Chief Constable? Fyfe remembered the manicured fingernails.

'Can you tell us anything about him, sir?'

'Not a lot. His wife died just over a year ago. Val didn't let it get him down. He took on a whole new lease of life after the event. His firm is relatively new but very well regarded. How he came to be at a murder scene in fancy dress is a complete mystery. I can hardly believe it. I've been trying to get Gregor. Don't know where he is.'

'We're trying to raise his other partners now,' Fyfe said, presuming it was being done.

'I had a bad feeling about this one from the outset. It's going to be messy. I'm glad you're there to watch over it.'

'We'll sort it out.'

'Good. Keep me informed – and congratulations, by the way.'

'Congratulations? For what?'

'You won the star prize in the raffle at the outing.'

'I did? What is it?'

'Dinner, bed and breakfast for two at Gleneagles any night you like.'

'So there is some justice, after all.'

Fyfe stood up and rapidly worked out his plan of action for regaining control of the situation. He phoned Sapalski but got a constantly engaged tone. He phoned Matthewson at head-quarters and got Randolph's home address and the background story of how the anonymous woman had phoned in to the radio programme with the name. It had been confirmed by the finding of Randolph's car in the street next to Zena McElhose at Wardie Avenue. Just because Randolph was a pal of the Chief Constable didn't mean he wasn't a murderer. In Fyfe's cynical eyes it damned him that little bit more. One person's embarrassment was another's entertainment.

Hilary appeared beside him. She had washed her face and done something to her hair. She smiled at him so appealingly the urgent need he felt to get away instantly evaporated. Sapalski was capable of doing everything that required to be done. Why couldn't he simply go back to lying with Hilary and pretend nothing had happened? This was the moment intended for the letter of resignation he had prepared earlier.

'I've got to go,' he said reluctantly.

'Are you okay to drive?'

He nodded. She was offering him an excuse to stay. He was probably just over the limit. He should wait until he sweated it

97

out of his system. But she didn't really mean it. She was helping him on with his coat. She wanted him to go, so that he could come back another time and be her sleeping partner again. He could take her to Gleneagles Hotel for a night. That was a classy option to have up his sleeve.

She hung on to his arm as they went down the stairs and kissed in the doorway. He put his hand under her T-shirt on the small of her back and let it rest on the waistband of her jeans. His next problem would be what to do with Angela, Hilary's black dress *doppelgänger*.

'I've got to go,' he said.

'Promise you'll come back.'

'You don't get rid of me that easily.'

Fyfe held her by the wrist and carefully wrote his phone number on the inside of her forearm. When he had finished he bent down and pressed his lips against the softness of the flesh. He kissed her hand and backed away down the path. The security light came on, holding his shadow ahead of him, draping it across the low hedge and on to the pavement and road. By the time he reached his car the shadow had shrunk to nothing. He looked back. Hilary's door was shut and the light in the sitting-room had been switched off.

25

Sunday, 18.37

Maureen Gilliland drove through the city silently, cruising inside the darkly warm cocoon of the Mercedes. She had no conception of where she was going, or that she was even moving. She kept her eyes fixed on the boundary carved from the darkness by the headlights. Instinct made her react to junctions and traffic lights, but in the main she was oblivious to the physical actions she was performing.

Occasionally she would notice where she was and what she was doing: one hand on the steering wheel, the other on the gearstick, feet resting on the pedals, accelerator pressed down, speedometer needle turning, raindrops on the windscreen, red warning lights on the dashboard for low fuel and an unfastened safety belt. But it was like seeing a landscape briefly illuminated by a shaft of lightning before it was plunged back into invisibility and she was being borne along effortlessly on a magic carpet of powerful, supercharged emotion. She had blanked out the encounter with Gregor Runciman outside the office. Instead, Val was beside her, his fingertips caressing her thigh and pattering like a small animal's feet across her stomach and up over her breasts, under her chin and into her mouth. He was whispering in her ear, telling her how much he loved her, telling her of the things he wanted to do to her, embarrassing things, terrible things, disgusting things, indescribable things, that made her shiver with the thrill of anticipation. And he kept promising that soon, very soon, the whole world would know the truth about their loving relationship. The irrefutable documentary evidence, the final vestiges of their mortal lives, was laid out to be found. People would talk about them in hushed voices. 'Who would have believed it of our Maureen?' they would ask each other incredulously at the office of Randolph and Runciman. 'I don't believe it,' they would say at the church.

But they would believe. They would have to believe. They would have no choice but to believe because the facts would be staring them in the face. Inescapable, unavoidable facts that revealed how she and Valentine Randolph had been lovers. She sucked at the fingers in her mouth, tasting a sickly sweetness. They could carve it on the headstone above her grave.

The wheel was abruptly wrenched from Gilliland's grip as the front offside tyre mounted the pavement. She grabbed it with both hands and turned it back. The entrance to Val's garden opened in front of her, human shapes fled from the parabola of light sweeping the ground ahead of her. The stone gatepost slammed into the side of the car. Her door burst open and the darkening evening roared in, damping the side of her face with its rain, terrifying her with its inhuman babble of noise. She stamped on the accelerator and the car leapt forward. The impulse of momentum closed the door, restoring the silence, shutting out the outside world. The car struck something else, forcing it out of the way.

The frontage of Val's house was directly in front of her, frozen in the headlights. There were cars across the steps to the main door, people moving around them, faces turning to watch her.

Red spots glowed on the bottom fringe of her eyesight, spilling their colouring upwards, splitting the fat drops of water on the windscreen into spectral rainbows. Val's hand tightened on her thigh, his mouth closed over her throat preventing her breathing. Her right foot was hard to the floor. The house rushed at her, inflating to gigantic proportions, and in the fraction of a second before she collided with it she realised there was no one beside her in the car, that she was alone as she had always been alone. In that instant her elation was transformed into blind terror and she screamed as the silence exploded around her with a deafening blast like a pin-punctured balloon.

26

Sunday, 18.39
Fyfe had just been waved through the garden gate police cordon keeping the reporters and camera teams at bay when the red Mercedes smashed into the rear of his purple Volvo. The collision caused his head to whiplash. A sharp pain stabbed into his neck. His head butted the rim of the steering wheel. The car lurched to the left, flattening a border of small shrubs, ploughing into the soft flower bed, and coming to rest with a bump against a staked tree that was knocked thirty degrees from the vertical.

Fyfe staggered out of his car, rubbing his neck and running towards the scene of chaos twenty yards in front of him that was illuminated by floodlights set into the lawn. The Mercedes had accelerated fiercely once he had been pushed to the side and smashed head-on into the driveway pillar of the stone balustrade that lined the set of four steps leading up to the front door of the house. The cordon at the gates had broken as the Mercedes crashed. Reporters were circling the wreck. Photographers were taking pictures. Television cameramen were filming anything that moved.

The Mercedes, sideswiping two police cars on its way past,

had climbed half-way over the balustrade and stuck there, half tilted on to its side. The bonnet was crumpled and steam was blowing out from its edges. The windscreen was shattered but intact and bulging outwards. One front wheel was sticking out on a bent axle, still spinning but winding down slowly. The boot, with its yellow and black number plate VR 1, was untouched but as Fyfe approached he saw flames beginning to lick up from underneath it where the fuel tank was situated. There were people milling around the car. Some were trying to wrench open the driver's door which was jammed, others were at the front apparently trying to lift it up. The sight of the quickly fattening flames caused cries of alarm and a redoubling of effort. The Mercedes door came free suddenly and a woman's limp body fell out on to the gravel. Her face was smeared with blood a brighter red than the colour of the car. One shoulder seemed to be missing, the arm emerging from her torso low down. Fyfe took an ankle and helped to carry her to the grass where she was laid out on her back. A policeman knelt over her and began giving the kiss of life. Another thumped on her chest. A cameraman knelt by her feet, recording everything. A floodlight was directly behind them, creating a theatrical silhouette.

Fyfe turned back to the wreck. People were trying to pull a body out from under the front. They were screaming at each other because the body was trapped by the weight of the car and no one was sure what to do.

'It's Sapalski,' somebody said. 'He's been crushed.'

A fire extinguisher hissed loudly at it spread foam over the rear chassis, snuffing out the flames. Fyfe joined with half a dozen other people to push the car further over, breathing heavily with the exertion, straining to take the weight when the shout came for it to allow two officers to crawl in and drag Sapalski out with them. His clothes were dirty and torn but otherwise he seemed unharmed. There were two parallel scars on his chin but they were not bleeding. His eyes were only half open, or half shut, as if he had a bad hangover. He looked deflated. There was no width to his chest. No one bothered to give him the kiss of life when he was laid on the lawn. They had given up on the woman too. The faces of both dead bodies were covered by uniform jackets. Silver buttons sparkled in the harsh lighting. Sirens wailed in the distance. Dark shapes moved stealthily through the upward shooting beams, already flecked with the shadows of swooping gulls.

Fyfe stood transfixed. 'For fuck's sake,' he said over and over again. 'For fuck's sake. For fuck's sake.'

He didn't answer when somebody asked him if he was all right. He didn't answer when a young reporter with pink-framed spectacles asked him if he could explain what was going on. He turned his back when he noticed a camera filming him. He didn't want them to see the tears that were running down over his cheeks and into the corners of his mouth. He tried to wipe his face dry and saw blood on his trembling fingers. He hadn't realised he was bleeding. It was not much, hardly anything at all, flowing from a cut at the side of his eye, but at least it told him he was still alive.

27

Sunday, 20.35

What was he doing here? Fyfe had never met Wilma Sapalski before, never talked to her, never wondered what she might look like. Yet, for some instinctive reason he didn't pretend to understand, he had insisted on personally breaking to her the news of her husband's violent death. He hadn't particularly liked Sapalski. Then he hadn't disliked him, hadn't really thought much about it. But he kept thinking that if he had pulled rank and prevented Sapalski going home temporarily, or if he had not been sidetracked into a couple of lost hours by Hilary, the investigation would have moved more quickly and Sapalski would not have been standing at the foot of the steps when the suicide driver in the Mercedes came roaring up the drive. He would not have been in the wrong place at the wrong time.

A few seconds either way and the car would have smacked harmlessly into a stone wall. Maureen Gilliland would still have died but that was what she wanted and her death would have been the end of it. Sapalski, saddened by the unnecessary loss of life when he himself was about to bring new life into the world, would have seen to the paperwork and gone home safely to his pregnant wife. Instead, the chain of chance circumstance meant an unborn child would never know its father.

'Why him?' Wilma wailed. 'Why my John?'

Good question, Fyfe thought. Bereavement training for police officers warned that such deceptively reasonable questions should not be answered directly for fear of getting embroiled in an impossible philosophical discussion. Be practical, be sympathetic, be understanding, be supportive was the advice, but leave the metaphysics and the spiritual stuff to visiting clergy or bleeding heart social workers.

Pregnancy had puffed up Wilma's face. Her hands and ankles too were bloated. Fyfe could see two fingers with deeply inset rings that were almost concealed by the puffiness. Her hair was lank and greasy and she had very little make-up on. Yet she had a vibrant quality and an inner confidence about her that transcended her physical condition and made her look very attractive. It was the glow of approaching maternity. At least she had looked attractive before Fyfe knocked on her door, broke the news and put out the internal lights.

He was well practised in telling women they had become widows. Angela had been one of them, all those years ago. She hadn't been pregnant at the time when husband Mike splattered his brains over walls and ceiling rather than give himself up. But there had been a smile on her face when she opened the door to Fyfe. It had faded rapidly. He had been practical, sympathetic, understanding, and supportive. They had ended up in bed together and forged a bond that he could not break.

Fyfe tried not to stare at the huge mound of Wilma's belly but it exerted a cruel fascination on him. It trembled every time a sob wracked her body as though the baby contained inside her was shivering with equally inconsolable grief. Fyfe stood helplessly, watching Sheila Grant, the policewoman delegated to accompany him, do all the comforting and the patting on the back. There was nothing else he could say or do. No point in telling her what a great guy Sapalski had been. No point in saying he understood how she felt because he didn't have the slightest idea. No point in claiming she would get over it because she might never get over it. Wilma would be allowed to weep for a while then Sheila Grant would gently coax her out to formally identify Sapalski's broken body. Fyfe had stood beside the doctor as corroborative witness when Sapalski's life was pronounced extinct on the lawn. Human emotion had to be overcome, bureaucratic procedures had to be followed and as a result there was no point in Fyfe doing anything more here.

'I told him to go,' Wilma was saying. 'I told him to get out. I was very selfish. He wanted to stay with me but I wanted to be alone. Why didn't I let him stay with me?'

'It's not your fault,' Sheila Grant repeated like a mantra. 'You must not blame yourself.'

'Why didn't I let him stay?'

'You must not blame yourself.'

'I could have stopped him.'

'It's not your fault.'

'I should have stopped him.'

'Don't fret.'

'He would still be alive.'

'There, there.'

'Why him? Why my John?'

'It's not your fault.'

Wilma held her swollen belly and wept despairingly. Fyfe turned away, anxious to escape but careful not to appear hasty. Bill Matthewson was waiting for him in the squad car outside. There was another bereaved woman to be visited, not a widow this time but a mother. Close enough. Every man had to be some mother's son.

28

Sunday, 21.16

What was he doing here? Fyfe had thought it a good idea to keep busy, to do the rounds and wrap up the inquiry. If he had to justify the way he spent his time on the evening Sapalski died he could give an itinerary of his movements, ending for the time being with this visit to the woman driver's elderly mother who sat red-eyed and breathless in an armchair stroking the black and white cat on the tartan rug covering her lap. A walking-stick was balanced against the arm of the chair. She was confused. She slowly shook her head, unable to take in what she had been told about her only daughter, her freshly dead daughter.

'Mrs Gilliland, did Maureen's recent behaviour lead you to think something like this was likely to happen?'

'I didn't suspect a thing. I don't believe it.' She tutted like a schoolmistress rubbishing a tall story told by one of her pupils. 'Are you sure it's my Maureen, not someone else?'

They were sure. Her younger brother, listed as next of kin on Gilliland's kidney donor card, had already identified her. He said he didn't believe it either even with her laid out in front of him. The organ donation was nipped in the bud too. Her body was needed for further examination, given the circumstances, and could not be tampered with.

'Were you aware of her love affair with Mr Randolph?' Fyfe asked her elderly mother.

The mother looked at him, closing one eye as though sighting on him down the barrel of a rifle. She looked right over the head of policewoman Anna McGrory who was kneeling in front of her holding her hand.

'No,' she said finally.

'Not even a suspicion?'

'No.'

'Did she have other boyfriends?'

'She never had anything to do with men, not since she grew up. I always assumed Maureen was . . . you know.'

'What?'

She lowered her voice, casting a glance over at the kitchen where her daughter-in-law was keeping out of the way. 'Not interested in that kind of thing.'

'Even though she was in her forties?'

'Oh yes. She looked after me. With her work and that, she said she didn't have time for a social life.'

'So you didn't know about Mr Randolph?'

'She sometimes mentioned him, I think. He was her boss, you see. His personal assistant. It was her job. They were members of the same church. St Andrew's. Do you know it? It's such a nice church. I used to go every week but I don't get about so much now.'

Fyfe put on his best sympathetic expression. He knew Mrs Gilliland was hiding her pain below a display of civilised politeness, or it might have simply been shock. He had tried to explain about the murder of Zena McElhose and Valentine Randolph being in hospital and then Maureen dying in the car crash, but he wasn't sure she was absorbing the information properly. He hadn't told her the car was crashed deliberately, sealing the fate of one innocent bystander, John Sapalski.

It was several seconds after she first mentioned St Andrew's Church that he realised McElhose had been a member there as well. So had Randolph. The connection between the threesome was reinforced. Maureen Gilliland would not be the first secretary to indulge in a bit of secretive hanky-panky with her boss. Nor would she be the first dutiful daughter to deceive a mother who would rather not know about her ageing offspring's sexual habits. Zena McElhose would not be the first lonely widow to find solace with a widower who failed to inform her he was knocking off an equally lonely spinster. Lust among the pews, playing footsie during the hymn singing, lascivious glances when heads were bowed for prayer, jealousy festering. Amen to that. Fyfe hoped he would be as rampant as Randolph when he reached his age. And he also hoped he would be able to avoid the divine retribution that had broken their unholy triangle.

The room was dimly lit and smelled musty. A fireplace of smokeless fuel was burning low, yellow flames licking round the nuggets of fuel like ghostly cats' tongues. The real cat clawed with a hind leg at its collar, scratching the old woman's hand and drawing a thin thread of blood. It jumped to the floor when she let go of it. Fyfe handed her a paper tissue. She ignored the bleeding and used the tissue to dab at her eyes.

'It's a new collar,' she explained. 'He's still getting used to it.'

'Of course,' Fyfe said in pretend small talk. 'What's his name?'

'Maureen called him Randy. It's Norwegian apparently.'

'Is it?'

There was a better case for its origin being closer to home than that. A cat substitute for the foot of her bed when Randy Randolph the boss wasn't available. Fyfe tried not to smile and began to worry about what might happen next once he extricated himself from Mrs Gilliland's living-room. Every off-duty officer was being recalled to ensure that the situation didn't get out of hand. Sir Duncan, back from Gleneagles to act the omnipotent Chief Constable, was handling the media personally, going on

106

television to show how seriously the force was treating the whole situation. Yet what crime was there left to investigate? Randolph had as good as confessed to old Zena's murder in the letter conveniently displayed on his study desk for the next casual passer-by to find. Gilliland's convincing imitation of a suicide bomber after borrowing Randolph's Mercedes clearly demonstrated her complicity to any jury with half a brain between them. She had discovered Randolph's fling with Zena, demanded he end it, and flipped her lid when she heard the news about the murder. The things that went on behind the closed doors of polite society. She must have known it was Randolph straight away, and with him being caught there was no one to wait for so she decided to end it all in a blaze of glory. In fact, rather than the alternative of fading away into lonely and unloved old age, she had died gloriously. Give her the benefit of the doubt and call Sapalski an unfortunate accident. Not her fault at all. If Randolph, Gilliland and Sapalski had been citizens of Greece it would be called a tragedy.

'It was her birthday tomorrow, you know,' the old woman said, her voice quavering with sorrow to a degree that was almost comical.

Fyfe knew. The personalised birthday card to his only true love had been found in Randolph's office. Presumably it was ready to be handed to Maureen when she arrived for work with a perfunctory peck of a kiss so office gossip would continue to ignore the relationship. The card was more jam on the thickly spread circumstantial sandwich. Intriguing too, that the call to the radio programme had been made from the phone box outside the Randolph and Runciman office. And how to account for Randolph's curious cupboard full of neatly labelled treasure hunt clues?

'She would have been forty-three tomorrow. Imagine. My baby, such an age, such an age for my little girl.'

The grieving mother sobbed quietly while Fyfe began to make his excuses and prepared to leave. The son and daughter-in-law entered as he stood up. They exchanged meaningful looks with him that meant they accepted the transfer of responsibility. Anna McGrory stayed on anyway.

The cat rubbed itself against Fyfe's leg. He bent down and smoothed the fur on its head and neck. It arched its back and

purred. He hooked a finger under its collar and lifted it on to its
hind legs as if he was testing its weight.

'Good boy, Randy,' he said stupidly. 'Good boy.'

It took a cynical bastard to look beyond what was staring them
in the face at that particular moment and Fyfe was looking. Why
did someone dress up in overalls, balaclava and surgical gloves
to inform a lover it was all over between them? Was it a question
worth asking? They already had enough answers to give an
acceptable solution. Why make work for himself? Why make
work for anyone else? Why bother?

29

Sunday, 21.17

Ramensky screwed up his face and swallowed the rum he hated
so much. It slid down his throat like melting tar reminding him
of hot summers and sticky tarmac roads that gripped the soles
of training shoes and made a soft ripping sound as they were
torn away.

'Don't you think you've had enough, sir?'

He was sitting at another bar in another pub. A young man's
face was looking into his. Above a bright red shirt and black bow
tie, it had raised scar tissue on the right cheek and above the
right eye which also had a slightly swollen lump underneath it.
The nose was broken and the ears were all squashed out of
shape. Jagged edges of jet black brilliantined hair hung over his
forehead like shark's teeth. And yet in the midst of this battered
and deformed facial package, the human teeth were perfect.
Ramensky stared curiously, watching them appear and disap-
pear behind the moving lips. They were evenly spaced and
beautifully white and seemed to be totally out of place. The teeth
had to be false, but they gave the impression of being natural.
How was it possible for a face such as this to take so many
knocks and retain its teeth in such mint condition? Ramensky
contemplated the conundrum and pushed his empty glass forward, indicating that it should be refilled.

'Don't you think you've had enough, sir?'

It was a reasonable question. Ramensky knew he had drunk more than enough in purely physical terms. He had already thrown up twice and the way his stomach was churning it would not be long before he did so again. But couldn't this guy with the perfect teeth understand that he was beyond the physical? He wasn't drinking to destroy his body, but to destroy his thoughts. He wanted to stop his brain working. He wanted to stop himself thinking because the guilt over Lorna, and now the idea that he might have killed old Zena, was becoming intolerable. It was rising to a crescendo and he could see no way of avoiding it. So he drank, the liquid equivalent of banging his head against the wall. And somehow his thoughts managed to survive fully formed to torment him and so he kept drinking. He couldn't even get drunk properly.

'I think you've had enough, sir. Why don't you go home now?'

Ramensky shook his head slowly. 'I should have done it, you know,' he said sadly. 'I saw the man. I went to see him. It could have been arranged, he said. Why not then, I said.'

'Of course, sir.' A consoling hand patted his arm. 'Come on, friend. Time to go home.'

'Too late now though.'

'Yes, it's late.'

Ramensky stared at the set of perfect white teeth and was suddenly aware there were two other people standing behind him. He straightened up slowly and turned his head to see them. They were red-shirted clones of their colleague on the business side of the bar, big muscular guys but still nowhere near as big as Ramensky. One was glowering at him, the other was smiling with malicious pleasure. He had a short wooden truncheon in his hand, the leather strap wrapped round his wrist, with *A Present from Malaga* carved on it. The other customers in the pub had retreated to a safe distance leaving plenty of empty space.

Ramensky returned the smile. This was a situation he could understand. This was what he had been waiting for. The blow of his head against the wall that would split his skull and let all his thoughts leak out and drain away. He turned back and hunched over the bar.

'No trouble now, friend,' the teeth said. 'There's the door. If you walk out no one will get hurt.'

Ramensky had eased his hand inside his coat and got hold of

the neck of the bottle of Black Bush whisky. He had been drinking it while wandering the streets, falling asleep briefly in a close where the bitter cold wouldn't allow him to lie for long. There was a little whisky left in the bottom of the bottle, but hardly any. He had had more than enough to drink anyway.

'I saw the man,' he said. 'I saw the man.'

'Have it your way.'

Ramensky drew the whisky bottle out as if it was a gun from a shoulder holster but his movements were ridiculously slow and cumbersome. When he swung it backwards with his arm the red shirts easily dodged out of the way. The bottle slipped from his grasp and hit a wall mirror end on, shattering it, causing a rainfall of broken glass and prompting the sound of female shrieking and scrambling feet. The truncheon hit him on the side of the head, knocking him backwards. He didn't feel anything but a dull, distant thump. He was still on his feet, a hand up to his head in self-defence. Blood was running into his eye and down the side of his nose. When he breathed in he tasted blood. Somebody was hitting him in the kidneys. There were hands on his neck, pulling his hair. He swung a punch but made no contact. The truncheon smacked into the other side of his head making a cracking sound, like a well-struck golf ball. He went down on his knees and somebody kicked him on the chin, making him bite his tongue. That hurt him the most. He fell on to his side and curled up as the blows continued to rain down on his head and back. Unconsciousness came only gradually.

30

Sunday, 21.49

The lighting in the empty police canteen was surreal. Mostly it was in darkness except for a wash of pale moonlight through rain-flecked windows and overhead strips in the adjoining kitchen sending down beams that looped round the abandoned glass and stainless steel serving counters and bounced off the formica-topped tables. Somebody had suggested they come down to the basement rather than stand around in the main crime room with Sapalski's empty desk sitting there like an open grave.

One of the big illuminated vending machines among the row of four was flashing a personal morse code message. It looked like the lounge of a sinking ship with tables and chairs thrown about haphazardly as it listed, throwing the assembly of detectives down into a single corner. Superintendent Les Cooper was at the centre of the group, still in his golf clothes, with everybody round him in a ragged circle. He was holding some paper in his hands. The others mostly had little white plastic cups. Fyfe stood on the fringe, concealing a yawn that rose from deep inside him, thinking childhood memory thoughts of how the gathering resembled a scout troup watching a knot-tying demonstration.

'The parrot bookend was stolen from Sir Duncan's home,' Cooper was explaining. When everybody looked blank he added: 'Sir Duncan, our Chief Constable. These are his initials, that is probably the date on which it was stolen, and the other numbers appear to be the code for disabling his alarm system. He tells me he had noticed the pair of bookends was gone and wondered what had happened to them, but it really seemed too trivial to worry about.'

Fyfe grinned with the rest of them but it was quickly overtaken by a puzzled frown. The top notch lawyer Valentine Randolph, it seemed, had a curious sideline breaking into his friends' houses. So far the owners of the bookend, the tin opener, and the cat's flea collar had been identified. All, bar Sir Duncan, were members of St Andrew's Church. The tin opener was the minister's. The collar was from Randy, Maureen Gilliland's cat. The paperweight belonged to the church organist.

Why Randolph did it was anyone's guess. Maybe he got a buzz from it. Unless there was another cupboard still to be found, it had been going on for just under a year, starting soon after his wife died. A lifetime of legal correctness, rounded off by a few evenings of illicit thrill seeking. Nothing bad, of course, since Randolph was an honourable man. Nothing harmful or unpleasant. Just a spot of breaking and entering and the theft of an object of small value and importance. If a householder noticed it was gone he was hardly likely to call in the police. Who would bother for a missing flea collar, or a tin opener or a bookend? Come to think of it, where was the other parrot bookend?

111

It made sense of the overalls and the balaclava and the surgical gloves, and it confirmed the motive to an extent. Old Zena must have disturbed him in the act. He had grabbed the mallet and felled her. The adrenalin rush then hit him like a runaway truck and his heart couldn't take the shock so he keeled over as well. When Marianne Dunne stumbled over the bodies the secret was out. Except the love note left on his desk didn't quite fit in with the scenario. If he was knocking off old Zena why break into her house all dressed up? Maybe it was part of the games they played? Or maybe he meant to frighten her? Maybe he had already told her their affair was finished and then hoped to get a hard on by going back and pinching a bauble? Or maybe when he went back he really did mean to murder her?

Fyfe's phone rang. He extracted it from his pocket and backed away from the circle of shirt-sleeved men, bumping against tables as he went, scraping table legs over the floor, attracting annoyed backward glances.

'It's me. Hilary.'

'Well hello. Long time no see.'

'I saw you on the television news. Are you all right?'

'I'm fine. Never better.'

They must have got pictures of him at the crash scene, Fyfe realised. He hoped they hadn't managed to catch him off guard and film the tears he had shed. That wouldn't do his reputation as a hard bastard any good at all. It was nice of Hilary to be concerned. He would love to cry on her shoulder.

'Are you sure you're all right? It looked nasty.'

'It always looks worse than it is. Believe me, I'm fine.'

'What was it about?'

'Who knows? People's lives fractured into a thousand bits. We're just trying to make sense of it now.'

'You're still working, are you?'

'I'm afraid so.'

'We can all sleep safely in our beds tonight then.'

'By ourselves?'

'By ourselves,' she answered with what sounded like a regretful sigh.

What was she trying to tell him? He sensed that she wanted him back for another friendly bundle on the sofa then, without a word being said, she would lead him through to the bedroom

112

and into her bed where they would sleep safely together. The prospect appealed to him hugely but he didn't think it was the right thing to do with his colleague Sapalski slowly stiffening on the mortuary slab. There was another reason too. He wasn't ready for Hilary. He knew it was Angela that was causing him to hesitate. Shag in haste, repent at leisure. How he was repenting now that Angela had her claws in him once again. Hilary was a warning to him, another temptress. Was it possible that she and Angela were sisters, separated at birth but with some kind of telepathic link that made them look so good in little black cocktail dresses? He noticed the other detectives were filing out of the canteen, stepping into a bright white rectangle of light flooding in from the corridor that made them look like aliens boarding their spaceships.

'You're not feeling sad, are you?' he asked.

'Not so much sad as lonely.'

'I'm stuck here for the night.'

'Oh.'

'Sorry. I'd come round but I just can't get away.'

'Pity.'

'A great pity.'

'What about lunch tomorrow?'

His stomach turned over. Was this deliberate? Maybe Hilary and Angela were working together, like co-stars in an Alfred Hitchcock movie plotting to drive the leading man insane.

'I can't do lunch, not tomorrow. I'm booked, I'm afraid.'

'Oh.'

The sprinkling of truth in his carefully constructed pack of lies made him sound as if he was playing far too hard to get. He had to relent or he would lose Hilary, and that was the last thing he wanted. He was imagining the recent touch of her fingers on his face, the soft pressure of her breasts against his arm, and the darting of her tongue against his teeth as they kissed.

'I'd like to see you though.'

'Tomorrow?'

'Yes. I'll call you.'

'Please.'

'I can't have you being sad and lonely. I've just got to get this case out of the way.'

'I'll let you get on with it then.'

'Okay. See you soon.'

'See you. Call me. I'll be waiting.'

The phone beeped as the connection was broken. Fyfe turned and found Sir Duncan Morrison standing at a discreet distance waiting to speak to him. He was, Fyfe judged instantly, too far away to have overheard. There was somebody else Fyfe didn't recognise beside him, a tall man looking round the room like a nervous, over-awed child.

'Just checking in with the wife,' Fyfe said.

'Here you are then.'

Fyfe took what was handed to him. 'What's this?'

'Your voucher for a night at Gleneagles Hotel. Be sure you and Sally enjoy yourselves.'

'We will.'

'This is Gegor Runciman, Val Randolph's partner. He's only just found out what's been happening.'

Fyfe offered to shake hands but Runciman didn't seem to notice. He looked awful. His suit was creased and the knees were stained. His naturally sallow skin appeared to be a veneer of light varnish over a bloodless surface below. Fyfe put it down to the shock of hearing about the death of a long-standing friend.

'Small accident,' he said illogically. 'I'll get over it. We were at school together, you know.'

'We were?'

'Me and Val. Known each other all our lives.'

'It must be terrible for you.'

'And Zena. I knew Zena. She was our client.'

Runciman nodded as he confided the information and stared wildly as though expecting Fyfe to say something significant. Fyfe wondered if the shock of Sapalski's death had affected him as badly as Zena McElhose's death, apparently murdered by his old friend Randolph, had affected Runciman. He hoped not.

'It's been a long day for both of us, David. We'll get a chance to speak to Gregor properly later. In the meantime I think we'll let the next shift carry on and come back fresh in the morning.'

'Sounds good to me.'

'Right then. Let's all go home.'

31

His two black labradors met Fyfe at the front door, capering and jumping about him as he came in to search for enough cash to pay the taxi driver. It was close to midnight. Sally, sleepy-eyed and dishevelled from bed, had to come downstairs in her floppy bunny slippers and search her purse while the driver waited in the hallway with Jill sniffing curiously at his trouser leg and Number Five growling at him from a safe distance. Finally the money was scraped together and a receipt was written out in exchange. The cab backed out of the driveway and the rattle of its diesel engine quickly faded into the night. The silence of the countryside descended round the house.

'Where's the car?' Sally asked.

'A minor accident,' Fyfe replied, not wanting to have to explain. 'Nothing serious but I may have bent an axle by running into a flower bed.'

'Are you all right?'

'I'm fine.'

'Are you sure? Let's have a look.'

'I'm sure.'

'How bad is the car?'

'A little out of shape but I'll probably get it back tomorrow.'

He rubbed his neck. It was a little stiff. When he bent over to pat Jill's head he had to think twice before straightening up. Too sudden a movement caused a bristling of needlepoint warning pains. He wanted sympathy. He wanted uncritical physical contact. He wanted Sally's fingers to knead his joints and knotted muscles, but he didn't want the bother of explaining all that had gone on. Sally obviously didn't know about Sapalski and he knew that, even if she did, she wouldn't ask many questions. She never did, he thought gratefully, as she inspected him for signs of injury.

'Hungry?' she said when she was satisfied there was nothing too badly bent or broken.

'No. I'll survive.'

'Coming to bed then?'

'That sounds an attractive proposition.'

Sally watched as Fyfe undressed and climbed in beside her, moulding himself to her shape and her warmth, an arm round her stomach, knees tucked into the back of her legs. He kissed her neck and her sweet-smelling hair and held her tightly to him with one arm round her breasts and the other round her stomach. She fell asleep quickly.

He loved her madly, he thought, thinking back reluctantly to the ashen faces of Wilma Sapalski and Maureen Gilliland's mother when they learned the news of the deaths of their loved ones. He couldn't imagine how he would react if it was his turn to answer the door and find some sad-eyed policeman saying how sorry he was but ... He and Sally had come a long way since their schooldays when they used to hold hands and snatch kisses between sessions of maths and geography. A teenage bust-up separated them for a few years but it seemed inevitable they would marry. Then came a beautiful baby, followed years later by an adult bust-up, divorce, rival lovers to taunt one another with, and back together again as if they had never parted. It seemed so natural, a process that had to be gone through to reach a certain point in time. This point. He had asked her to marry him again a dozen times. It was her who was reluctant, not him. He didn't understand women.

Fyfe squeezed Sally against him, enjoying the feminine warmth of her along the full length of his body. He loved her. Whatever he did, he would always be in love with her. If it was always like this, he would happily stay and be safe here with Sally. But it couldn't always be like this. Things changed. People changed. Times changed. Angela upset the balance of his hormones and his reason. Now Hilary was about to do the same thing to him. He believed in predestination as a good excuse for explaining his inability to stay on the right side of the line. Life, his life, was a relentless process of constant change. The process was continuing.

The dogs lay at the bottom of the bed, heavy weights pinning his feet down. He closed his eyes and tried to sleep but kept seeing John Sapalski's lifeless body contained inside an oval of luridly green grass on the lawn in front of the big house. And all

116

around Sapalski in their own exclusive little patches of green were other dead bodies he had seen, images of death stretching back down the years like stepping stones across a vast expanse of water. And when Fyfe looked up again there was Angela standing in among the bodies in her fur coat, smiling at him so suggestively and holding out her arms to invite him into the refuge of her intimate embrace. It was an offer he knew he was powerless to refuse.

He turned on his back, and then on his side away from Sally. He found a position for his head that relieved the mild stiffness in his neck. Then he turned on to his back again. At the foot of the bed, almost invisible, Jill raised her head and looked at him. For a long time he tossed and turned, moving in slow motion lest he do himself an injury, unable to keep his eyes closed for more than a few seconds at a time. Dead people closed their eyes and never opened them again.

He slipped out from under the covers, careful not to disturb Sally. She didn't wake. He put on the same clothes he had just taken off and tiptoed out of the bedroom with his shoes in his hand like a thief in the night. Jill and Number Five followed him downstairs, obediently quiet, rib cages rubbing against his legs. He put on his shoes and tied his laces. He found a torch in the kitchen and, carving a pathway through solid black with the sharp-edged cone of light, walked out to the wooden shed at the bottom of the garden.

The floorboards were old and warped under the clutter of boxes, garden tools, and an old tumble drier wedged into the corner that appeared in the torchlight. He locked the door behind him and shifted the drier out of the way. Going down on his knees in the space he had created, he prised a section of short-cut boards up with the help of a paint-spattered screwdriver. The dogs sat beside him watching as the boards gave way reluctantly, edges sticking in the channels and holding them stiffly at a sixty-degree angle. The torch, balanced on a wooden strap on the side wall, showed a huddle of more than a dozen tin boxes. They lay like makeshift coffins about a foot under the surface, all different sizes and shapes. Some were faded tartan with pictures of castles and men in tall wigs, others were plain, one was long and narrow with a picture of a rose-fringed cottage among a riot of flowers on the lid. He picked it out and eased it

117

open with his thumbs. The banknotes that were exposed seemed to swell out of the confines of the box. There were purple twenties, rusty brown tens, and blue fivers all piled on top of each other. The dogs leaned their heads forward to sniff inquisitively at the incriminating evidence.

Fyfe took out a handful until the pile subsided below the box's rim. He counted what he had in his hand, three hundred pounds' worth, and slipped the notes into his pocket. He sat looking down for a long time, ignoring the cold that crept over him, recalling the moment when he had taken the money from Angela and turned criminal. No turning back now. That was the problem with predestination. Once it had run its course, it was impossible to correct the mistakes that were made along the way.

He had been so calm about it, driving home with the cash in the boot, leaving it there overnight and only panicking in the morning when he realised just how easily he could be found out. He had found the tin boxes in a cupboard in the cellar, mostly the legacy of Christmas and New Year gifts of shortbread and chocolates, and packed the banknotes into them. He had agonised for ages over where to hide them. The shed was so obvious, yet so convenient and there was no reason whatsoever for anyone to suspect he had the money anyway. So he lifted the floorboards and scraped out a hole and buried his ill-gotten loot with the same sense of guilt as if he had been secretly burying a dead body.

Several times Fyfe had considered doing a Lady Macbeth and washing his hands of the crime by burning the notes and getting rid of all trace of them. He had never done it, of course. The very idea was obscene to him, closely followed by the alternative of packaging it all up and sending it to a deserving charity. Money wasn't flesh and blood, it didn't scream when it burned, but it had rights too. It existed in its own right and it had within it so much potential. It was, after all, better than any insurance policy or pension plan. If it ever proved necessary, it could easily keep Fyfe for the rest of his life. That was the beauty of it. That was why he kept the cash and couldn't get rid of it. That was why he had to risk it. If, one day, he was to be found out, so be it. That was why Angela was able to order him to come to her, and he had no choice but to obey.

Fyfe took a single note and examined it carefully. It was a

Royal Bank of Scotland twenty with a picture of Brodick Castle on one side and an eighteenth-century guy with a big nose and a curly wig on the other. It was old and creased and dirty and faded from passing through thousands of different hands.

'What do you think, my dogs?' he said. 'Will we carry out a small experiment under carefully controlled laboratory conditions?'

Jill and Number Five sat panting quietly. Fyfe held the note by a corner between finger and thumb and took the cheap gas lighter he used for lighting other people's cigarettes. He turned it to high and produced a tall flame that created huge shadows and was reflected deep inside the dogs' eyes. The flame jumped on to the hanging corner of the note and rapidly grew fatter and wider as it blackened and consumed it. Fyfe waited until the flame was at his fingertips, a pinprick of heat in the shed's block of cold, and dropped the final piece. The flame was snuffed out in mid-air when it ran out of usable fuel to burn. The dogs' bright eyes vanished. The light from the torch was pale and watery. The remaining thin strip of black ash drifted down, twisting and rocking from side to side in tantalising slow motion until it reached the floor. There Fyfe ground it to an unrecognisable powder under the heel of his hand.

'One's enough,' he said. 'Don't you agree?'

Fyfe replaced the biscuit boxes in the hole, pulled the floorboards down and stamped them firmly back into position. He pulled the tumble drier back into the corner and scattered other stuff around to restore the appearance of dusty disorder.

The torch batteries were running out fast, the beam waning and narrowing. By the time Fyfe reached the back door of the house it was virtually useless. He went into the new conservatory to sit in one of the wide armchairs, inviting Jill and Number Five to lie on him to keep him warm. He sat looking up through the glass ceiling at the stars beyond a diaphanous veil of cloud and played his favourite game of trying to predict the near future. What would happen with Hilary? What did Angela want? But, like the torch batteries, his energy was fast running out.

The next thing he knew Sally was shaking him awake and the dogs were jumping to the floor. He shook his head to clear the fuzziness and flexed leaden muscles.

'Are you deaf?' Sally was saying, holding out his phone. 'It's been ringing red hot for ages.'

In the chair Fyfe looked at his watch but couldn't focus. He had no idea what time it was but noticed the sky through the glass ceiling was definitely lightening. Threads of cloud straggled across his field of vision like broken veins across an eyeball. It was McInnes at the hospital, Fyfe's dulled brain realised at the second attempt. Things must be moving.

'Don't you ever sleep?' Fyfe said.

'I can't. My contract of employment expressly forbids it.'

'What do you want?'

'You asked me to call if there was any change in John Doe's condition.'

Fyfe's brain struggled to think who John Doe was. It came to him slowly. For McInnes, John Doe was the original anonymity of Valentine Randolph. His balaclava man must have regained consciousness. Now they would be able to get the full story, to explain away all the niggling inconsistencies and discover what was really going on when the meat mallet connected with the side of poor old Zena's eggshell skull. Randolph would provide the truth.

'What's the change? Has he come round? Can he talk?'

'He has just undergone emergency surgery.'

'And?'

'Remember I told you I wouldn't bet on him recovering?'

'I remember.'

'Well, it looks like I won the bet.'

'What do you mean?'

'He's a non-runner.'

'Dead?'

'He's dead.'

'He won't be talking then.'

'That was my diagnosis too. You should have been a doctor.'

Sally was standing over Fyfe holding out a mug of coffee. Her hair was a designer mess. There was a red mark on her cheek where something must have been pressing against it. She was wearing her floppy bunny slippers and her legs needed shaving. She looked highly desirable. Fyfe decided he had two options, the more appealing of which was to go back to bed with Sally.

'What is it, David?' she said. 'What are you doing down here?'

'Business. What else?'

'A big case?'

'Yes. The murder.'

'You're not coming back to bed then?'

'I've got to go back in.'

'What? Now?'

'Afraid so. Can you call me a taxi?'

32

Monday, 06.38

Sandy Ramensky came round slowly, viewing the yellow-painted walls and scrawled graffiti with detached inquisitiveness. A single light bulb burned above his head, hurting his eyes when he looked at it, making the aluminium toilet and wash-hand basin in the corner flicker and blink as if they didn't really exist. Ramensky was fully clothed and lying on his side on top of a thin mattress that gave little or no cushioning from the unyielding surface underneath, and covered by a coarse blanket that smelled of stale urine and worse. He couldn't feel the shoulder that was taking his weight. His toes inside his socks were very cold. He had the impression each was frozen solid and hanging off the end of his body like icicles on the edge of a cliff.

Ramensky moaned despairingly. The alcohol was still in his blood, narrowing the veins, restricting the oxygen supply to his limbs and his brain, causing a pulsing pain to beat behind his eyes like the thumping beat of a bass guitar. He knew he was in a police cell but he had no memory of what he had done or what had happened to him the night before to get him there. With his free hand he patted the tender bruises on his face, discovering that it was swollen and out of shape. The last thing he remembered was leaving home; a kiss for Marianne, a loving glance at sleeping Lorna, and out into the night. It had been quite a while since he had gone on a drinking binge seeking the utopian state of oblivion.

'How's the head, chum?'

A policeman in a white shirt was leaning over Ramensky. A smoothly featureless face like a ball of putty looked down, split at the bottom by a grinning crescent mouth. Keys jangled loudly. Distant laughter trickled in through the open cell door. Ramensky put his hand over his eyes and squeezed. The shock of fresh exterior pain briefly cancelled out the aching inside, then merged with it. He tried to open his mouth but found his tongue was uncomfortably large and tender. His dry lips were stuck together, so the only sound that emerged was an unintelligible grunt.

'Have a good night then?' asked the jolly jailer. 'Want to tell us any more about your personal problems?'

Ramensky hid behind his hand. A frigid coldness spread along the length of his body as he desperately tried to recall what he might have said. Was it possible he had let slip the secret that might condemn him? Had he poured out the content of his troubled soul? Had he revealed his guilt? It was the kind of thing he tended to do. Was another putty-faced policeman called Fyfe on his way to this very cell to check the confession he had made overnight? Fyfe didn't know he was wrong in his assumption, couldn't be told. Who would believe a drunken madman who knew he was doomed as soon as he saw Mrs McElhose stretched out dead? He could tell his version of the story but no one would believe it. He didn't know if he believed it himself. Perhaps his conscience had invented an alternative version of the truth so that he could live with what he had done?

'How about beginning simply? How about a name?'

Ramensky moved his hand and the harsh electric light stimulated the pain buzzing round his head. He put the hand back over his eyes and tried to speak. A flashback came to him of a mouth with perfect teeth, hands grabbing for his wallet, the sickly taste of sweet dark rum. All three things overwhelmed him and were impossibly real for an instant, then they were gone. He was back in the cell, wrapped in muscle-tightening cold, his head pounding as though he was beating it against the wall. He moaned again and tried to sit up. It was a difficult manoeuvre. He reached out for support, swinging his feet down off the platform bed. His shoes were already on the floor. The laces had been removed. The policeman took his arm and steadied him in a sitting position. Ramensky held the blanket over his shoulders.

'Come on. Tell us your name. There must be somebody worried about the state you've got yourself into.'

Lorna's pale face with its huge innocent eyes appeared in his mind. She might be dead already, gasping for her last breath in this world to be taken while her hopeless father was snoring off the drink. The doctors had said the final relapse could come at any time. He and Marianne had sworn she would never be left alone. At least Marianne would have been with her at the end.

'What did I do?' Ramensky managed to say, not recognising the thick sibilant voice that produced the words.

'A little bit too much to drink,' the policeman said. 'A small disagreement with the management of the drinking establishment you were patronising and an assault upon their persons.'

'Did I do that?'

'By the look of you they gave at least as good as they got.' He had opened a notebook and was waiting with a pencil held against the blank page. 'So are you going to end the mystery and tell me your name?'

'Will I be charged?'

'The boss reckons you've had enough punishment. The pub doesn't want to cause a fuss. I don't want more paperwork. We've checked your prints and they don't match any outstanding warrants. Looks like it's your lucky day.'

'What time is it?'

'Half an hour before the end of my shift.'

Ramensky breathed deeply through his mouth. His secret was probably known to the murder investigation team by now. Fyfe was aware of it anyway and the rest were bound to have found out. When he hadn't turned up for work, that would be the clincher. They would be out now hunting him on the streets; tracker dogs and helicopters and 'Wanted' posters showing the face of the dangerous murderer. They probably wouldn't think to look in their own cells. As soon as he gave his name it would be all over. They would have their man.

'Go on. There's nothing in your wallet to say who you are. Give us your name and you'll be on your way home inside an hour.'

'Ramensky,' he said, feeling as if invisible thumbs were squeezing a deep-seated splinter from his brain. 'Alexander Ramensky.'

The policeman regarded him without rancour or even curiosity. He began to write in his notebook. Ramensky bowed his head in resignation.

'I bet they call you Sandy.'

'Yes. They do.'

'How do you spell Ramensky? Have you got an address?'

Ramensky spelled out his name and told him his address. Another flashback came to him; strong whisky, Van Morrison music, the carved legend of *A Present from Malaga* arcing towards his face. It made no sense to him. He shook his head and instantly regretted it because his brain seemed to slap about like a sodden sponge.

'That's fine then, chum,' the policeman said. 'Put your feet up again if you like. Don't worry. We'll have you out of here soon.'

He went out, leaving the cell door open. Ramensky stared after him, shivering, knowing that it could only be a matter of time before they appreciated who he really was and slammed the door shut on him for good.

33

Monday, 07.20

Fyfe dozed in the back of the black cab on the way back into the city, forced to put on the seat belt and tighten it radically to prevent himself sliding about. The driver, a huge man in a Russian-style fur hat that was crushed against the roof, drove far too fast on the empty roads and didn't let up on the bends so that centrifugal force pushed Fyfe from side to side until he clamped himself in one corner with the belt. The driver talked at the same speed he drove, tossing subjects back over his shoulder in the hope that his passenger would take him up on one. Politics, sport, religion, the price of potatoes, bankrupt millionaires, the theft of charity boxes from pubs; the entire range of stories culled from recent newspapers.

'See that old wifie that was done in yesterday,' the driver said. 'That kind of thing would never have happened a few years ago. It's the schools I blame. They don't teach respect any more. No respect for their elders. I would bring back hanging. There would be more respect in this world if we stretched a few necks now and again.'

Fyfe didn't argue with him. He occasionally made noises out of politeness to pretend he was listening but the torrent of unwanted conversation washed over him. He sat with his eyes half closed, rolling his neck slightly to ease its stiffness. He thought back to the drunken philosopher at the party telling him about Zeno's paradox and the impossibility of travelling the distance between two points and actually arriving. He had died in the night and this was hell, he thought, trapped in the back of a black cab with a garrulous driver on a journey that never ended.

Then there was Ramensky's homespun idea about transferring the spark of life that kept old Zena McElhose alive to his dying daughter, and Hilary's throaty giggling as she asked how much it would cost to hire a contract killer. There was an obscure pattern in all this, a combination of disparate events somehow designed to steer Fyfe in a certain direction. And he could see where it was leading him, straight towards one Donaldson MacDuff, the local godfather everybody knew to go to if you had a need to get rid of someone for whatever reason. And the intriguing element, potentially the final piece of the pattern, was MacDuff himsef attempting to get in touch with Fyfe. Was it just coincidence? If not, maybe sometime in the future he would have a philosophical conundrum named after him. Fyfe's Vexation?

'Which number was it?' the driver asked.

The taxi was entering a long street of terraced houses and a jumble of hedges and fences. It was the street where Hilary lived. Fyfe, wondering where to go, had asked to be taken to her address. He looked up at the first-floor living-room and bedroom windows as the taxi cruised sedately past. The curtains were drawn. Behind them she was lying alone. He would have liked to go up there, climb into bed beside her and mould his body against hers. But it wasn't going to happen. They still had to go through much more of the mating ritual before they got to that

125

stage. What he had planned to do was knock on the door with a bottle of milk and a bag of fresh rolls and demand breakfast. But he was already changing his mind when Sally had sleepily kissed him goodbye with the easy familiarity of long acquaintance, casually stroking the inside of his leg in a gesture of shared intimacy. Then looking through the rear window to see Sally on the doorstep with the two dogs beside her, a snapshot of domestic bliss and happy families. At his own home, he told the taxi driver to take him to Hilary's but he knew then it wasn't where he meant to go.

'Change of plan,' Fyfe said. 'Do you know the Soft and Gentle sauna parlour?'

The driver stopped the slow-moving cab and turned round in his seat. His bushy eyebrows rose and merged with the fur hat. 'Soft and Gentle? Sure I know it,' he said disapprovingly.

'Take me there then.'

It wasn't far. A five-minute trip in the near-deserted streets with not a person to be seen among all the greyness and litter swirling in the wind. The city looked like a set for a post-holocaust film. The driver had lapsed into silence, probably preparing a diatribe on loose morals to be inflicted on his next passenger. The Soft and Gentle had basement premises on a steeply sloping road that had a classic view of the castle from the pavement and a licence to open from 6 a.m. To cater for early risers, was the local joke.

'Bit early isn't it, mate?' the driver said, accepting the fare through the open window of the cab.

'It's an emergency,' Fyfe replied. 'Matter of life and death, you might say.'

34

Monday, 07.51
Ramensky walked past the entrance to his own home with his head down and his hands deep in his pockets. A white and orange police car was parked outside it, and another one further down the drive at the big house. No one was about. He should

have been back from work a few hours ago. Marianne would be beginning to get worried about him. Lorna would be sleeping peacefully, doped up by her latest dose of medication, dark blue veins showing through the parchment white skin of her little arms and legs.

Ramensky stopped, turned on his heel and marched past his home in the other direction. If a policeman came out now he would give himself up, tell the whole story and hope for the best. He would tell them how he didn't have the guts to go through with his crazy plan. They wouldn't believe him, of course. The man hadn't believed him. He had laughed. So what? What could they do to him? Could they hold a gun to his daughter's head and threaten to kill her unless he told the truth they wanted to hear? No, but they could put him in prison and prevent him being with his daughter when she died. They could do that.

Ramensky stopped again, turned, marched back. The strength and coldness of the wind were making his eyes water, driving tear-tracks over his cheeks like slimy slug trails. He could hardly believe what was happening when they threw him out of the cells earlier that morning, handed him his shoe laces, trouser belt, and other belongings in a big brown paper envelope, patted him on the back and wished him well. They simply didn't realise who he was, having failed to make the connection. He tried to tell them but his swollen tongue made it difficult for him to speak properly and they just smiled patronisingly, thinking he hadn't fully sobered up, and hurried him out the door. He fully expected to feel the toe of a boot on his backside to hurry him up as he went.

It might happen again if he tried to explain himself here, except that Marianne would recognise him and the police would have to listen. But Marianne would be furious that he had turned to drink. She would shout and rage at him, hit him, but then she would do what he feared most; she would ignore him. She would sit in the armchair, cuddling Lorna close, staring into space, and hum tunes with no beginning and no end. It frightened him to see her like that.

He opened his mouth wide and let the freezing air in at his swollen tongue. It acted like the touch of a cold cloth on a fevered forehead, drawing out some of the dull pain. His head was still sore, his badly bruised face still tender, his legs weak, his whole body fragile. He couldn't face Marianne in this condition. What he needed was a drink. That would help him to think more clearly and decide what he should do next. He had money. His wallet, retrieved from the envelope, proved to have survived the night better than him. Explanations could wait.

Ramensky closed his mouth. He stopped, turned, marched away. He didn't look back.

35

Monday, 08.10
Edinburgh Castle loomed on the skyline at the top of the hill. The steps down to the entrance of the basement sauna parlour were edged with wind-battered shrubs in heavy pots. A pale neon sign saying *Soft and Gentle* hung over a set of narrow double doors. Only one side was open. Fyfe's shoulders were too wide for the gap. He had to turn sideways to pass through into a vestibule with an interior door in front of him and a hotel-style reception desk blanked out by a broad expanse of glass striped by alternate lines of opaque and clear. He saw somebody move behind it, a barely recognisable human shape that was continuously broken up and re-formed as it rippled over the lines of glass.

'Good morning, sir,' said a husky voice. 'Welcome to the Soft and Gentle. Do come right in. Just push the door.'

Fyfe did as he was told. The door opened stiffly, held back by the thick carpet on the floor beyond. On the other side was a surprisingly large area like a doctor's waiting-room with chairs and sofas against the walls and a central low table piled with magazines. A wide-screen television with breakfast television presenters mouthing silently was suspended from the ceiling in one corner. There was a low buzz of extractor fans and a mumble of piped music just audible over the burble and hiss of a coffee-making machine. The wallpaper was red and black, like the aftermath of a bad accident. Framed pictures with individual spotlights were either erotic or abstract; it was hard to tell with a cursory glance. At least three corridors and two closed doors led off the space. Elaborate plaster cornices vanished into walls showing where the partition walls had been constructed.

Two women stood up and flashed professional smiles from behind masks of make-up and glossy lipstick as Fyfe entered. Both had sun-lamp tans. One was small and well endowed, standing unsteadily on high heels, wrapped in a nurse-style uniform of short skirt and tight blouse. The other was taller, slimmer, wearing similar high heels, short skirt and blouse. She sucked deeply on a cigarette and released the smoke from the corner of her mouth in a controlled stream that was almost a contemptuous gesture. Fyfe liked her instantly and wanted to rescue her from all this. He smiled back.

'What can we do for you, sir?' said the smaller one.

'Quite a lot probably,' Fyfe replied, looking straight at the tall one. 'But I'm afraid I'm already on duty so I'll have to pass.'

'Are you sure? I'm Selena. This is Patricia. We're here to make sure you have a good time. Anything you want we can provide.'

'I'm sure you could but at the moment I've got business with your boss, Mr MacDuff. It would please me greatly if you informed him I was here.'

'Who are you?' Selena asked.

'David Fyfe.'

'Does he know you?'

'Oh yes.'

'Is he expecting you?'

'Oh no.'

'I'll see if he is in.'

Selena disappeared down one of the corridors. Patricia sat down, crossed her legs and sucked deeply on her cigarette. Her body language spoke volumes about Fyfe as a time-waster who was denying her the opportunity to earn quick commission.

'Business good?' he asked.

'No.'

She opened out a newspaper on the adjacent chair and leaned over to read it. A colourful Page Three girl flaunted her chest among a few short paragraphs of black and white text. Fyfe looked down at the magazines. They were all soft porn. He picked one up and flicked through the pages. A female body made up of many different parts writhed and twisted and contorted in the rush of images. A succession of changing faces leered out at him. He thought he caught Patricia watching him even more contemptuously. He got a fright and dropped the magazine when a fat man grabbed his arm.

'David, my friend. How good it is to see you.'

'Morning, Donaldson.'

'Come to my office. Have you had breakfast? Have something. I'm having a couple of rolls. Would you like one? Selena is just going to run to the carry-out for me.'

'A black pudding roll would be nice.'

'With brown sauce?' Selena asked.

'Please.'

MacDuff kept hold of Fyfe's arm. He pulled him along a corridor into a tiny, windowless office decorated with the same brothel wallpaper, stuffed with filing cabinets and dominated by a wide desk that split it in half. He half climbed, half squeezed round the edge of the desk and flopped into the swivel seat that squeaked in protest. Fyfe sat in the chair opposite him. The only object on the desk was an old-fashioned adding machine with a long tongue of cash-roll paper looping out of it.

'Before we get down to business will you tell me one thing, Donaldson,' Fyfe said.

'What do you want to know?'

'Do you really get punters coming in here at this time in the morning?'

'Of course.' MacDuff leered obscenely. 'Sexual desire does not conform to a strict timetable. Lust comes upon us at any time.'

'I suppose you're right.'

'I am. Look at that.' MacDuff pointed and Fyfe turned to see one of four red lights illuminated above the door. 'First of the day. That's Patricia in her cubicle and earning her keep.'

'That should put a smile on her face,' Fyfe said.

'She's good. She will certainly put a smile on his.' MacDuff's mood changed in mid-sentence. 'You didn't tell the girls who you were, did you?' he said anxiously.

'I told them who, not what.'

MacDuff considered the statement carefully and nodded. 'It's just that they get nervous if they know the police are around.'

'So do I.'

'How did you know I would be here anyway?'

130

'I know everything about you, Donaldson. We have hidden cameras recording your every movement.'

For a second MacDuff looked wary and uncertain, then he realised it was a joke and he laughed, gurgling like a partially blocked drain. Fyfe sat back in his chair. MacDuff was the biggest crook in the city but, apart from a couple of promptly settled parking tickets, didn't have a single conviction. Not even any youthful indiscretion to blot his record. He was an unscrupulous and highly successful entrepreneur in a specialised area of business covering sex for sale, protection rackets, and debt enforcement. He was only in his mid-thirties but already looked two decades older. He was dissolute, overweight, and unrepentant, rather relishing his physical resemblance to Marlon Brando in his role as the Godfather, complete with wheezy voice, puffy face, and inevitability of dying of a heart attack before too long.

'So what can I do for you, David?' He used a handkerchief to dab at the sweat on his forehead that had been brought out by his short journey to collect Fyfe from the reception area.

'You were looking for me, Donaldson. I am the mountain come to Mohammed. Or is it the other way around?'

'Oh yes.' A look of annoyance came and went. MacDuff scowled at his chunky silver watch. 'I was drunk. I tend to do stupid things when I'm drunk.'

'Don't we all.'

There was no formal deal between the two of them, no question of payment either way, although this was not the first time they had sat facing each other in the cramped, seedy office. MacDuff fed Fyfe with discreet and occasionally useful nuggets of information on low-life intrigue because he liked the sense of power it gave him. Fyfe offered him nothing in return except the illusion of having a tame DCI on a string. He had covered up the episode of the cocaine in the cubicle because he knew the blame would be delegated down on to the girl who worked it and the poor girl was already having a hard enough time. He didn't care how MacDuff had interpreted it.

'It's about the killing of this dear old lady,' MacDuff said.

'I thought it might be.'

'Why did you think that?'

'No reason. Just a hunch. I am senior investigating officer on the case, after all.'

'Are you?'

'Somebody has to be.'

'Anyway, it's about this lady.'

'Mrs McElhose.'

'That's her. How old was she?'

'Seventy-three.'

MacDuff shook his head sadly and looked at the ceiling. His eyebrows squashed themselves together in the area directly above his nose as though they were being sucked down a hole there. 'Three score years and thirteen. I'll never see that kind of age.'

'Neither will I,' Fyfe agreed.

'People who live to be as old as that deserve respect. The Chinese respect their old. All the Orientals do. My mother lives with me. She's over seventy. I look after her well.'

'What's your point, Donaldson?'

'You're not wired up to record this, are you?'

'Not as far as I know.'

'I should have you frisked.'

Fyfe held open his jacket. 'Get one of your girls to give me the once-over. Just don't send me the bill afterwards.'

MacDuff shoved the tip of his little finger into one nostril and rotated it through two hundred and seventy degrees. He pulled it out and examined the end. At that point Selena arrived. When she opened the door it banged against the back of Fyfe's chair. She was carrying the lid of a cardboard box holding the rolls and cups of steaming hot coffee. She leaned over to lay it down on the desk and Fyfe got a flash of the back of her thighs right up to the buttocks. He couldn't make out whether she was wearing knickers or not. She left without saying a word. MacDuff seemed to have forgotten about his idea of having Fyfe searched. He checked the paper bags and handed one to Fyfe. The black pudding was hot and the sauce tangy. Milk wasn't an option for the coffee because there was none. It burned his throat.

'This bloke comes to me and says he wants somebody bumped,' MacDuff said through a mouthful of bacon and egg.

'Why would anyone ask a fine upstanding gentleman like yourself such a question, Donaldson?'

'Beats me. Happens all the time. Anyway, this bloke has made a big effort to find out the rules and customs because he's not a native in my universe if you understand my drift. So I see him, thinking it will be some insurance job or the like.'

'Very public-spirited of you.'

'Look, I'm being straight with you, Chief Inspector. Give me a break, will you?'

Fyfe took a telling. 'Sorry,' he said.

'So he's sitting there where you're sitting now and he's a big ugly bastard. His head is almost touching the roof and I've got a couple of boys on the end of the alarm ready to burst in if he turns nasty and I can hardly believe my ears when he tells me he wants this dear old lady bumped and he's saved up ten thousand pounds to pay somebody to do it.'

'Not a big enough fee, Donaldson?'

'I don't do old ladies. It's not right. And he told me all about her, how she was a widow and how she did the flowers for the church and how she was so nice and wouldn't harm a fly. He was very strange.'

'And what did you do with him?'

'I told him it wasn't possible. He didn't argue. Just got up, thanked me for my time and walked out.'

'Did he tell you the name of the woman he wanted killed?'

'Yes, he did. That's why I recognised it in the paper. McElhose. The poor old dear. If I'd known I could have prevented it.'

MacDuff's eyes were watering. He stuffed a fist into his mouth and bit on it, wiping some egg yolk from his bottom lip. Fyfe screwed the paper bag that had contained his roll into a ball and tossed it back into the box lid. He drank some more coffee, burned his throat again. He finished his roll in four bites.

'Did he give you a reason for wanting this old lady dead?' Fyfe asked.

'He said he would inherit something valuable from her.'

'What?'

'He didn't specify. I didn't ask. I assumed cash.'

'Did he tell you his name?'

'Yes.'

'What was it?'

'It was a foreign-sounding name but he had a local accent.

Ramensky. Alexander Ramensky. Polish probably. I had him checked out because I thought it could be a set-up. It wasn't. No form. No nasty friends.'

So Ramensky had followed up his theory and checked out the practical possibility of having Zena McElhose's life swapped for little Lorna's. If Donaldson MacDuff had moral qualms about such a deed, there would be others who would overcome them for ten thousand pounds. Many anonymous drinkers in late-night bars down by the docks would be glad of such lucrative work. And even if he didn't find anybody, or if he didn't have the money, he might have steeled himself to do it personally. Needs must when the devil drives and your only child's close to death. It would be simple to break into the big house and finish off old Zena. Then there was the slight hitch of coming face to face with balaclava-clad Valentine Randolph who is indulging in his cheeky weekend habit of stealing knick-knacks from under the noses of friends and acquaintances. Or he might have seen Randolph breaking in and seized the opportunity. Whichever, Randolph comes off worse. His heart can't take the shock. He collapses unconscious presenting the perfect opportunity to be fitted up as the murderer. Zena's paradox is explained and then Randolph dies without regaining consciousness and Ramensky thinks a guardian angel must be looking down on him, if not on his daughter Lorna.

'You'll testify to all this in court, won't you, Donaldson?'

'No.'

'You'll give a formal statement?'

'No, and I'll deny this conversation ever took place if I have to. I have my reputation to think about.'

'Why bother telling me then?'

'You needed to know. I'm telling you because I don't like people who inflict violence on innocent old ladies. It could have been my mother, for goodness sake. It makes me sad.'

'Well, it's just as well I've got it on tape then.'

MacDuff stopped in mid-chew, one cheek bulging. His eyebrows were once again sucked into the hole in the middle of his forehead.

'Just joking,' Fyfe said and MacDuff started chewing again. 'Thanks for the coffee and the roll.'

'Are you going to arrest Ramensky?'

134

'I'm going to speak to him.'

'What about the guy in the hospital you found? Was he on a contract? Are you absolutely sure it's this Valentine Randolph, the fat cat lawyer?'

That had been MacDuff's real point in shopping Ramensky. He thought the man he rejected had found a rival operator willing to take on the job. That would be enough to give him indigestion; a rival selling services on his territory. And that was why he had phoned in originally. The fact that Randolph was who he was confused the issue nicely.

'It's him all right.'

'What was he playing at?'

'We'll probably never know. He's dead himself now.'

MacDuff sniffed. 'So there is justice.'

'Of a kind.'

'Glad to be able to help,' MacDuff said. 'We don't need people who bump off old ladies out on our streets.'

'How true. Don't get up. I'll see myself out.' Fyfe rose to leave. 'One thing I'd like to know, Donaldson.'

'What's that?'

'The going rate.'

'The rate for what?'

'For a contract. The rate to bump somebody.'

'No old ladies?'

'No old ladies. How much?'

'Depends. Of course, all this is speculation. I'm not able to say for certain, being a respectable businessman.'

'Naturally. But what's the average price?'

MacDuff pouted, fingering his adding machine, taking on the role of cost-conscious accountant. 'Four thousand for some damage maybe, a few broken bones. Five to six for serious damage, hospitalisation. It can be a bit like the legal aid system. Your income will be taken into account.'

'I'm on the poverty line. What about terminal damage to someone in the right age group?'

'Ten thousand.'

'Very reasonable.'

'But for you, Chief Inspector, I'm sure a substantial discount could be arranged.'

Fyfe turned to the door. 'That's nice to know.'

36

Sir Duncan Morrison hadn't personally arrested anyone for – he thought about it for a long time – for at least fifteen years. Chief Constables were supposed to be above that sort of thing, above and beyond. It was a difficult matter of etiquette to decide how to handle the situation. His first thought had been to get Fyfe's advice but his mobile phone wasn't taking calls and he couldn't be contacted. Instead he had got on to headquarters and discovered the first person available was DS Graham Evans who never seemed to sleep. He hadn't explained fully, just told Evans what he wanted him to do, finding a degree of pleasure in keeping the information to himself and the entire police force he commanded in the dark. In his bedroom he raked around the sock drawer for the set of handcuffs he knew had to be somewhere in the house, but he couldn't lay his hands on them. He was, he realised, as excited as a schoolboy proudly handing in a particularly good bit of homework for marking. How often did a Chief Constable get the chance to lead by example? This would show them that he wasn't just a figurehead and pen-pusher. He had already worked out how to be suitably modest when the story was splashed across the newspapers and television screens. The public loved a reluctant hero much more than an arrogant pushy one.

Sir Duncan worried that he didn't have proper corroboration but Evans would provide that soon enough. He was troubled by a sneaking suspicion that he was being set up just as he was now being told Val Randolph had been set up for Zena McElhose's murder. If it was all a practical joke the world would laugh at him for being so gullible as to accept this bizarre story at face value without a shred of supporting evidence. But he hadn't accepted it yet, though he believed it. There was concrete evidence and Evans had gone to check that it did exist. That would be the ultimate seal on the confession.

Sir Duncan paced the dining-room, impatiently anticipating

Evans' return. He watched the big man sit doubled over, holding his head in his hands. He was sobbing inconsolably. He was not dangerous. There was no malice left in him. It had all been poured out. He was a totally broken man. He had been like that for the last fifteen minutes. There was no need for the handcuffs he hadn't been able to find anyway. Sir Duncan shook his head, marvelling at the twist of fate that had put the murderer on the chair and him in command of the situation. He held out a hand towards the big man. The long arm of the law, he thought. You're nicked, he almost said as he had seen them do on television cop series. But he didn't.

'Why?'

It was not the first time he had posed the question that morning. The response from the man in the chair was always the same: a bemused shake of the head.

37

Monday, 10.24

So where was Ramensky? Marianne didn't know. He hadn't gone to work last night. They had phoned up looking for him. He must have gone on the piss instead. Marianne wasn't angry. She seemed more disappointed that he should have left her on her own. She sat rocking in the fireside chair with her knees drawn up and little Lorna held to her chest. Fyfe sat dumbly in the corner of the warm sitting-room. The gas fire was on full, sucking the moisture and the oxygen from the air, but draughts round the window frame compensated. The curtains, still drawn against the daylight, moved sluggishly. Old Zena's granddaughter, Carole something, had arrived from the south and was in the house with Marianne. She was a dark-haired young woman with high cheekbones, a wide mouth, and a posh accent. Her eyes were swollen with crying. They looked as if they had been ringed with red crayon. She had formally identified the body that morning. Now she was on her knees in front of Marianne with her forehead resting on the arm of the chair. Lorna stared across at Fyfe, unsettling him. He began to bite at a ragged edge of fingernail on his thumb. He bit too hard, stripping too much away. A smear of blood appeared. He could taste it on his tongue.

Fyfe hadn't told the women why he had come, or what he had learned. As soon as he realised Ramensky was not there he had turned his visit into a matter of routine, just a check to see if there was anything useful Marianne had remembered since making her statement. Naturally there wasn't. He stayed because to rush away abruptly might have seemed strange, although the two women had withdrawn into themselves and mostly ignored him. Then he found himself trapped, trying to think of an excuse to leave, wondering why the conventions of polite society assumed such importance in the midst of such an unconventional situation.

On the way over to Ramensky's home Fyfe had contacted headquarters and spoken to Les Cooper to see what was happening. Randolph's death without regaining consciousness was common knowledge, and Fyfe's car was dented from the night before but mechanically sound, according to the police garage. The insurance would pay to have it straightened out. He could collect it whenever he was ready. Otherwise there was little to report except that Evans and Matthewson were following up some kind of tip-off and they had probably found the fountain pen Randolph had signed his farewell letter with. It was in Maureen Gilliland's handbag. Curious that. She must have stolen it from him.

Fyfe was glad Ramensky had gone on a drinking binge and put himself out of reach. He could understand that reaction. It was what Fyfe would have done. If Ramensky had been there, Fyfe doubted if he would have told him what he knew about his attempt to hire a contract killer anyway. Why should he be the source of more grief for Marianne and her dying child? Why should he deprive the family of its father at such a critical time? Zena McElhose had been old. She would have died soon anyway. If Ramensky helped her along in the hope of gaining benefit for his child, then who could blame him? Who could honestly say they would not have done the same thing themselves? It was stupid, superstitious nonsense, of course, but it might have worked. How was he to know until he tried? And if he didn't try how was he to know that it wouldn't work? And Valentine

Randolph was an entirely convincing scapegoat. Maureen Gilliland's suicidal final fling gave him the motivation and the credibility. There was no need to look beyond him. Ramensky's head on a plate was not required to produce a satisfactory solution. Good luck to him.

Fyfe looked at his watch. He had been here too long, he decided. It was time for him to put his own life in order as best he could. He would have liked to drop in past Hilary but she was almost certainly at work. He stood up, making a show of getting ready to leave. No one watched him except Lorna, her big eyes in the unhealthily pale face following his every step across the room.

The post-mortems would be well under way by now, lethally sharp knives zipping open the pasty white flesh. There would be little blood. It would have more or less dried up overnight. Pinkish liquid would leak out collecting like oil under a car, following the moulded channels of the stainless steel mortuary tables, running down to the open plug hole at the corpse's feet where, since they were in the northern hemisphere, it would turn in a clockwise spiral and drain away. Old Zena's skinny remains would be first up, then Gilliland, then Sapalski if he was being done in the same place. Randolph might still be warm by the time the pathologist in his rubber boots got round to him. The dead bodies were like buses, Fyfe thought. There were none for ages and then they all came at once.

'Don't worry,' he told Marianne. 'Everything will be all right.'

38

Monday, 10.35
It was an ordinary cupboard, known locally as an Edinburgh press, in the corner of an ordinary bedroom. The frame was sanded and varnished, giving it an appearance that suggested it should have a more important role and lead through to another room rather than into shallow storage space. There were doors like it in every bedroom. The key was in the lock.

To get to the press, Graham Evans moved a pair of suitcases

out of the way, and then a white chest stuffed so full of clean towels that the top would not close properly. The second-floor bedroom with its flowery wallpaper and utilitarian units was not as tastefully or expensively furnished as the others in the house. It seemed to be very much an afterthought.

'Well, what do you think?' Evans asked as he turned the key.

'I think this is our last chance,' Matthewson replied.

'Let's take a look then.'

He pulled the door open. Inside, at the bottom, was a neatly stacked pile of folded blankets and sports equipment. There were four narrow shelves, starting at waist level. Each contained an orderly line of objects and ornaments, two dozen in all, remarkably similar to the contents of the cupboard they had found at Randolph's home. The smallest was a red-stoned signet ring, the biggest was a sealed white jar of Stilton cheese, but the thing that instantly attracted both men's attention was on the front edge of the top shelf, a bookend in the shape of a parrot carved from soapstone.

'Fuck me, it's Hunky Dunky's missing parrot,' Evans said. 'How the hell did he know it would be here?'

'He obviously has friends in low places,' Evans said.

'He must know something we don't.'

'Presumably we will find out for ourselves soon enough.'

'And Hunky Dunky gets his parrots back.'

'Plus the glory. It looks like he's cracked the case all by himself.'

'God, he'll be unbearable now.' Matthewson put his nose right up against the parrot without touching it. 'Who would have believed it?' he said. 'Aren't the games some people play truly amazing?'

39

Monday, 12.15

Angela was waiting for him. Fyfe saw her, slightly distorted, through the patterned glass of the ten-foot-high revolving door guarding the entrance to the Caledonian Hotel. His bowels went rigid, making him stop. For a fleeting instant he considered turning and walking away. Then he moved forward again.

The doorman was standing in the shelter of the doorway. He was a big man, almost certainly ex-army, a sergeant-major probably, with a ruddy face and sprouting nostril hair. He was wearing a blue, knee-length tunic coat covered in a deluge of yellow and red braid as if he had spilled multi-coloured toothpaste down his chest. He had a blue cape round his shoulders and carried a half-opened umbrella ready to snap into full size to protect approaching residents and customers from the blustery sleet over the final few yards to the entrance. Fyfe hadn't qualified as a potential client for the hotel so he got right up to the entrance and was standing on the mosaic coat of arms on the ground before the doorman stood to attention and reacted.

'Good afternoon, sir,' he said, keeping his parade ground voice in check.

He bowed and tilted his black top hat which shone silkily as it moved. He pushed the door with his free hand so that it gathered speed like a fairground roundabout beginning another ride that would take Fyfe from one part of his complicated life into another separate but inseparable part.

Fyfe stepped into one of the four V-shaped compartments and followed it round. Angela came into sharp focus as he was disgorged inside the hotel. She was about twenty yards from him across the foyer, opposite the reception desk in a kind of dead-end of low-slung leather seats and sofas interspersed with vases of flowers on pedestals. She stood up and came towards him. Heads turned because she was something to look at; beautifully made up and expensively clothed in a long white wrap-around dress split to just above the knee on one side. Her breasts stood proud as if they had been carved with a whittling knife.

Fyfe met her half-way. They held hands, embraced. He kissed her on the cheek. She kissed fresh air beside his cheek. They stood back and looked at each other. Anyone watching them would have seen two old friends having an emotional reunion.

'Welcome back, Angela,' Fyfe said.

'Same to you,' she replied.

'How long's it been?'

'A little over one year.'

141

'Is that all? Can I buy you a drink?'

'Can you afford it?'

'I think so.'

'You've not blown all our money then?'

'Not it all.'

'That's useful to know.'

'Why? Have you?'

Angela laughed, throwing back her head and exposing a not-quite smooth throat in the way women were taught by specialist articles on how to trap your man in women's magazines. Fyfe knew he would enjoy flirting with her, had already enjoyed the look and feel of her body. She was attractive, dangerous, and forbidden. If he had to fill in a form for his ideal date those three qualities would be top of the list. And she didn't, he noticed with a tension-easing exhalation of relief, bear the smallest resemblance to Hilary. Apart from height and womanly shape, they had nothing at all in common. It couldn't be that Hilary was some kind of female Jekyll and Hyde, reading his mind and reviving his personal nightmare for the fun of it. They really were two separate women.

Angela looked older than he had expected, not worse just older. Like him, she would never see forty again and that personal landmark was fast receding in the distance. The face powder was thick, lines around her eyes breaking through it. The lipstick was thick too. The body was firm. Cosmetic surgery, he speculated? Breast implants? Inventively engineered underwear?

There was an air of contented sophistication about her. If he hadn't known her, he would have marked her down as a rich bitch who had come through hard times and landed on her feet with a rich husband, probably fat and balding, and her own bank account, probably very healthily in the black. But he did know her and there was between them this unbreakable bond forged the night they took the money and hurried away from a huddle of bloody bodies. Even without the money and the sex he could not have told on Angela. He really believed she hadn't killed anyone, and anyway he was hopelessly compromised the moment he helped her run instead of doing his duty and clamping on the handcuffs. It had been a momentary aberration, but a fatal one. Now he was stuck with bundles of banknotes under his garden shed and a woman who shared a secret that meant when she whistled he had to come running.

They went to the cocktail bar. She drank Martini, sipping from the glass delicately and leaving a transparent pink impression of her lips on the edge of the glass. He drank vodka and tonic so that it wouldn't be noticeable on his breath later. They ordered from a menu and waited at a table to be called through to the dining-room. Angela crossed her legs and the white dress clung to her tightly. She told him about her new husband, Felippe, the Spanish Euro MP, who was indeed fat and balding but endearingly besotted. He thought she was having lunch with an old school friend.

'Female naturally,' she said. 'Felippe does get very jealous.'

'Why didn't you tell him the truth?' Fyfe said.

Her head went back. The throat presented itself, displaying her vulnerability while she mocked him with her laughter. Fyfe laughed himself, well aware of his talent for asking daft questions. Angela looked down her nose at him and patted his hand affectionately. When you have been married four times, she explained, it is relatively simple to lose all recollection of one of those marriages. And so Felippe had no knowledge of the first unfortunate marriage to Mad Mike Barrie, the deceased professional criminal who was directly responsible for bringing Angela and Fyfe together more than a decade ago, and who was therefore also indirectly responsible for their renewed intimate relationship, and the lunch they were about to have.

'A funny old world, is it not?' Angela asked rhetorically.

'Paradox after paradox,' Fyfe agreed. 'I find them at every turn.'

'And secrets that only two can share.'

Summoned to their places in the dining-room, they settled into an alcove screened by dark wood and mirrored glass. The food was good if a little scarce on the plate for Fyfe's liking. The wine was good too, but a mistake. He could feel it combining with his lack of sleep, bubbling inside his skull to create a mad scientist's concoction that was transforming him from rational person to absurd misfit. He was supposed to be leading a murder inquiry. Instead here he was making eyes at a former lover and partner in crime. Surely that was a disciplinary offence. If ever there was a time to have his resignation ready in his pocket this was it.

Angela was easily the best-looking woman in the room. People who passed the table tried to be casual but let their glances linger just that second too long. Fyfe was walking on broken glass, hoping desperately that there was no one around to recognise him. If he had been wearing a hat and raincoat he would have pulled the brim down over his brow, turned up the collar to slouch away. Supposing somebody did recognise him and demanded an introduction to his lunch companion. The game would be over. Her name would reveal her history. The whole story would unravel irresistibly from there, connecting them, condemning them. He would be well and truly fucked. And yet there was no one among the forty or so spread round the other private alcoves, and the collection of tables in the centre of the dining-room. There was no one at all in this small crowded city where he had lived out his entire life who really knew who he was or what he had done. There was only Angela. They were a pair.

40

Monday, 13.04
Ramensky looked down and saw cars passing eighty feet below him. The shock made him take a step backwards but then there was nothing beneath his foot. He bent at the knee in an awkward curtsy, instinctively whirling his arms to restore his balance, realising he was standing on a narrow stone balustrade in a gap between buildings. He was high above a busy road on one side and six feet above the ground on the other. There was an Ooh and an Ah from the uneven string of people gathered in a semicircle on the pavement close to him as he gradually gained control and his jerky movements slowed and finally stopped. A traffic warden in an overcoat and peaked cap with a yellow band stood in front of them, half crouching, reaching out. Ramensky thought he looked as if he was a lone member of a barber shop quartet about to burst into song.

'Come on down, mate,' he said. 'Come on down. It can't be as bad as that. Come on down.'

A double-decker bus swept past at pavement level. Curious faces were pressed to the windows, looking back as the bus drove on. Ramensky felt the sleet-wet slipstream brush his face. He deliberately stood on one leg and pirouetted one full revolution, slipped and had to flail his arms again to stay upright. The pavement crowd went Ooh. The traffic warden clenched his teeth and snatched his hand back.

'Careful now, mate,' he said, sinking back into his former position. 'It can't be as bad as that now. Come on down.'

Ramensky scratched his head. He had no recollection of how he came to be on top of this wall. He was in the city centre, opposite the Central Library, at the side of the National Library, on George IV Bridge with the rat-run of the Cowgate, one of the original thoroughfares of the ancient city, tunnelling underneath him. And the alcohol was bearing down on him again, rearing like a giant wave about to crash over his head and return him to the oblivion he had inhabited since he had started drinking again that morning.

He was in a lucid period, but it was closing fast. He began to cry and didn't know why, only that he was afflicted by a huge and terrible sorrow that brooded over him like a pot-bellied vulture on his shoulder. He looked down into the Cowgate and the surface of the road seemed to slam up with sudden violence into his face. His head burred like the inside of a clanging bell. He jerked his head back and lost his balance again. Somebody grabbed hold of his arm. He snatched it free and danced a few tightrope steps away from the young bearded man in a dirty anorak who had tried to rescue him. The traffic warden was still down on one knee in front of Ramensky.

'Easy now,' he said. 'Let's not get too excited. Let's just keep our heads here or there's going to be a bad accident.'

Ramensky wiped the tears from his face with his sleeve. He wanted to die. That was why he had climbed up on to the wall. He intended to swan dive on to the road below. If the impact didn't break his neck, the next car along in the steady stream of vehicles would finish him. It was strange, he thought calmly. Suicide seemed such an attractive option for him. Death wasn't something to be feared, but something to look forward to. He would get there before Lorna, prepare to receive her so that she was never alone. It was a simple act. All he had to do was launch himself into the air. In a few seconds it would be over.

But he was losing it. The alcoholic haze was closing around him. He had to hurry. A police car had drawn up, wheels bouncing on to the pavement, scattering the crowd, spilling dark uniforms, peaked caps with black and white bands. The traffic was held up. No more buses. People in the roadway. Horns blew impatiently, sparking off echoes that made a trail into the distance.

Ramensky turned away from the crowd. A landscape of rooftops, turrets, and church towers spread out ahead of him. He raised his arms like a bird spreading its wings, went up on his toes. The wind slapped at his face, forcing him to close his eyes. It made his coat balloon out. It filled the sleeves, infiltrated inside his shirt, froze the bare skin of his chest. It lifted him off the wall into the air. He tilted his head, kept his arms spread wide, imagined he was flying as the cold air rushed past him. But then his knee struck something solid with a gentle bump like a child's playful kick. His arm was next, only a little harder, then the whole side of his body, and his cheek. It wasn't painful at all. He hardly noticed it, but when he opened his eyes and looked down the angle of the cars passing far below him had changed. He was looking directly down, hanging over them like a freefall parachutist. One passenger was hanging out a window looking up, shaking his fist, shouting angry words that were whipped away on the wind. A policeman's hat dropped past him. It bounced on the roof of a car and disappeared under the wheels of the following one.

He wasn't falling. He was dangling like a clown on the mobile above Lorna's cot. He twisted, turning, and saw that they had him by the ankles and were dragging him back up. His face was scraped against the rough damp stone. He searched for a grip but there were no handholds. They weren't going to let him die, after all. They weren't going to let him take the easy way out. He struggled half-heartedly but collectively they were too strong for him. He began to cry again, imagining his tears falling on to the cars below, a human rainstorm hammering on the metal roofs, creating a terrifying din that made the occupants cower in fear.

He wanted to die yet he was mightily relieved he was alive. The alcohol was closing over his head, drowning him once more.

His head was spinning. Everything was a blur. Before they got him back to the safety of the pavement he had lost it and blacked out.

41

Monday, 14.03
'What is it you want, Angela?' Fyfe said.

The lunch table had been cleared. They were drinking coffee from impossibly thin, almost transparent cups and finishing a second bottle of wine. Another mistake. During the meal they had inched round on the semicircular bench seat so that there was only a gap of six inches between them. Sitting almost shoulder to shoulder they were able to talk in confidential whispers.

'I wondered how long it would take you to ask me that.'

The coffee was strong and viscous; the handles of the cups were so delicate Fyfe could only lift his up by pinching it carefully between finger and thumb. His little finger stuck out at right angles. She smiled at him and picked up her cup. The fingernail on her pinkie was long and curved, manicured to a sharp point. Light reflected on its clear varnish, splitting the spectrum, creating a tiny rainbow that flickered in and out of existence as it arced through the air. Fyfe experienced a sympathy pain in the small of his back, feeling the point of that fingernail digging into his flesh and the hard muscles of Angela's thighs pressed against his, and her hair falling down on either side of his face screening him from the outside world as the partition walls round their private alcove now screened them in the public arena of the hotel dining-room.

'What are we doing here, Angela?'

'Where would you rather be?'

'What do you want?'

'Nothing. I thought it would be nice to see you.'

'Do you want money?'

An amused tinkling laugh belied the narrowing of her eyes and the tightening round her mouth. Was it pride? Disappoint-

147

ment? Sadness? Melancholy? Pity? Fyfe regretted his bluntness. He fiddled with the cuff of his shirt so that he could check the time. They were bound to be looking for him back at head-quarters by now.

'I don't want your money, Dave. You know that.'

'Just as well. I've blown the lot,' he lied, guiltily suppressing the memory of the bundles of notes in the garden shed from his nocturnal musings.

'I hope you enjoyed it while it lasted.'

'Oh yes. What did you do with your share?'

'I invested it then got myself a new husband to cover everyday expenses.'

'Very wise.'

Angela looked at him in a way that made his bowels coil into a painful knot. Sexual arousal was an inappropriate response for the circumstances but he couldn't do anything about it. He tried to cross his legs but his knee bumped the bottom of the table. Angela put down her coffee cup with aristocratic elegance. The rainbow balanced on her fingernail vanished and then reappeared as she raised her hand to her mouth. She shuffled her backside and moved even closer to him.

'Why do you think I asked you here?' she said softly.

'To blackmail me.'

'I thought you would think that.'

'Did you?'

'You have a poor opinion of people.'

'It must be the company I keep.'

'Why did you come?'

'To convince you I wasn't worth blackmailing.'

'How were you going to do that?'

He shrugged helplessly. 'Throw myself on your mercy?'

He looked down to see that Angela had laid her hand over his on the table-top. Five perfect fingernails shone above his stubby and ragged equivalents on the pristine white surface. There was a stain of blood on the side of his thumb.

'Do you want to know the real reason I asked you here today, Dave?'

'Yes.'

'To confess.'

'I'm not going to arrest you, Angela. I had my chance, remember.'

'It's a personal confession.'

'Go on then.'

'I like you, Dave.'

'I like you too.'

'If things had been different I could have loved you, Dave.'

Surprise clamped itself over Fyfe's mouth. He was lost for words. This wasn't what he had expected at all. It was getting too heavy and too weird for him. The pressure of her hand over his was becoming greater. He watched the bones ripple on the back of her hand and slowly relax. The weight on his mind was lifted. He was safe, he realised. She was fond of him and had no intention of turning him in. He would survive this in one piece. A waiter hovered, offering liqueurs. Fyfe waved him away.

'I've never really loved anybody,' Angela explained. 'Certainly nobody I've married. Not even Mike. I was too young, impressionable and infatuated. I know that now. I have the wisdom of great age.'

'You're not that old,' Fyfe said limply.

'I could have loved you though, Dave. If we had met when we were younger and unattached, unencumbered by cynicism and bad life decisions, we would have clicked. I would have wanted to have your children. I would have wanted to spend my life with you.'

'This is deep metaphysical stuff, Angela.'

'Have you ever wondered why you put your career on the line and prevented me from going to a prison cell?'

'I could never resist a damsel in distress.'

'Seriously, Dave. It was such an extreme thing to do.'

'For the money?'

'That wasn't it. You didn't even know about the money before you committed yourself.'

'For the sex?'

'No, not that either.'

'What then?'

'Because you could have loved me too.'

'Ah, right.'

'That was why you did it, you see.'

'I see.'

'Thanks.'

'Don't mention it.'

'We were a could-have-been that never was. You and I.'

'Pretty close though.'

'Not really. Not close at all.'

'Seems a shame when you put it like that.'

'Does it? There is something between us though, David.'

'Apart from this table, you mean.'

'A bond grows between two people like us. I don't know how you describe it. It's a bond, a fellow feeling that comes when a friend becomes more than that.'

'Becomes a lover?'

'Sex has a lot to do with it.'

'Of course.'

'It's very rare. Only some people experience it.'

'Like us?'

'Exactly like us. Do you feel that bond with me?'

She was touching Fyfe's forearm, lightly squeezing. There was a dreamy urgency about her manner that made him uncomfortable. He had never seen her in such a strange mood. It worried him. She seemed to age as he looked at her, suddenly becoming older, wiser, way beyond his understanding. He moved his neck from side to side to relieve the stiffness and hoped he didn't look as if he was shaking his head.

'It was something Billy said.'

'Who's Billy?'

'My third husband. He was a major in the army, set himself up as a mercenary when he was demobbed. He had very interesting scars.'

'Oh.'

'I always remember what Billy told me. He said when you see action and come under fire then the unique experience turns the people you are with into special friends. They are marked out from everyone else you might know. They're different. They've been with you in a life and death situation. You never forget that.'

'Yeah.'

'When we had sex it was like that.'

'Was it?'

'Not the first time, but the second time we did it. Remember, in your flat with the suitcase of money by the door. That really had an edge for me. How was it for you?'

Fyfe struggled to find a suitable answer. 'Pretty good,' he said.

'That moment when we climaxed was like being in combat. Don't you agree? Life and death were wrapped up in it because it was at the extreme. We were under fire. You saved my life. Don't you see, David? Don't you see?'

Angela was pawing at his forearm, demanding Fyfe look at her. He felt as if he should duck to avoid the volley of emotional intensity emanating from her. His face was burning from the gradual infusion of blood that had accompanied her description of sex as a form of warfare. He worried that she was speaking too loudly and other people would be able to hear. He agreed it had been an exciting night, the element of integral danger and illegality lending it an edge he would never forget. He certainly wasn't going to argue with her. He nodded and grabbed her hand before she scratched him and drew blood. She took it as a sign of affection and visibly relaxed, smiling beatifically as if she had reached a climax and slipped through into the afterglow. Fyfe was mentally measuring the space between him and Angela, imagining himself crossing to half-way, and then half-way for the remaining distance, and then half-way again, and again. Never reaching her. There was no paradox involved in this particular situation. It was the exception proving the paradoxical rule. It was the way things really were.

Angela ended the reunion abruptly by getting up from the table. She slipped her arm through Fyfe's and led him back to the reception area. She kissed him on the cheek and wiped off the lipstick mark with her thumb.

'By the way, how are your dogs?' she asked brightly.

'Fine,' he replied. 'Never better.'

'And your wife?'

'I didn't get round to marrying her a second time.'

'It must be true love then.'

'Something like that.'

'You're still together?'

'Up until last night anyway.'

'Take my advice. Keep it that way.'

'Will I hear from you again?' Fyfe asked.

'Maybe not in this lifetime.'

'After Felippe falls by the wayside?'

'Don't worry, Dave. I won't be making any claim on you.'

'I thought we were comrades in arms?'

'We were.' She laughed at some private memory. 'If I do ever come back it will be another lunch. Will you come?'

'I wouldn't want to miss it.'

'Good. See you around then, comrade.'

'And you.'

She kissed him and again had to wipe away the lipstick. Fyfe retreated through the hotel's revolving doors, watching Angela's white form fade away through the patterned glass. The doorman tipped his hat, motioned to a waiting taxi on the rank and stood aside when Fyfe shook his head. The rain had turned to sleet. It was whirling in long lines down Lothian Road, its whiteness vanishing into the darker wetness of pavements, roads and vehicles. A snowflake struck his cheek and slid over the skin like a razor-sharp blade slitting it open. He put his hand up, expecting blood but finding only melting snow. The shock of its icy touch seemed to wake him from a day-dream, but he could still taste the wine on his tongue. He blinked rapidly and started to walk, feeling himself dragged reluctantly from somewhere infinitely far away back into the harshness of the real world. He put Angela out of his mind and began to think about how he was going to handle the Ramensky situation. As soon as he turned on his mobile phone it rang. Matthewson spoke to him.

'We've solved Zena's paradox,' he said.

'Congratulations.'

'It wasn't Randolph.'

'I know.'

Fyfe realised they must have found out about Ramensky so the self-imposed dilemma of whether or not to protect him was gone, melted away like the snow off his face. Sadness mingled with relief that he no longer had to make a choice of what to do.

'Sir Duncan cracked the case, believe it or not. He's going to explain all to the team, make it a big set-piece occasion. Kick off is four. He's like a dog with two tails.'

'Is it rock solid?'

Fyfe hailed a free taxi. It braked hard, swerving in close to the side of the road just past him, spraying his trouser leg with slush.

'We have hard evidence and a signed confession.'

'And you did it all without me.'

'Afraid so. Want to know the details?'

'Don't spoil the chief's big moment. Where have you got Ramensky?'

'How the hell did you know about Ramensky? I was just getting round to telling you about him.'

Fyfe was in the back of the taxi. The driver was looking over his shoulder waiting for instructions on where to go. The wine in Fyfe's belly made him feel warm and contented. He was very pleasantly drunk.

'I'm a detective. It's my job. Where have you got him?'

'He's in the cells at St Leonards.'

'No one will object if I take a detour and visit him, will they? Maybe he will confess to me as well.'

'That would make things very interesting,' Matthewson said.

'Good then. See you at four. Book me a ringside seat.'

42

Monday, 15.09

Sandy Ramensky lifted his head and the yellow walls around him turned from vague fuzziness to rigid solidity. He sat up and the movement made the walls spin furiously. He had the impression he was at the centre of a musical carousel, surrounded by galloping ponies and smiling clowns' faces in a whirl of clashing musical chimes. Then the painted eyes and lips were abruptly wiped off one of the circling faces and he was looking directly at David Fyfe, the man who knew what he had done, who almost certainly knew exactly what he was thinking.

'I didn't do it,' Ramensky said.

'Neither did I,' Fyfe replied.

'I thought about it.'

153

'I know.'

'I went to see the man.'

'I know. MacDuff told me.'

'He threw me out.'

'So he says.'

'That was it. I didn't do it.'

'Didn't you?'

Ramensky blinked. The walls stopped rotating. The imaginary music stopped. He felt unshaven, unkempt, and sore all over. Fyfe was standing casually in front of him with his hands in his pockets, smiling slightly. He sat down on the edge of the bunk and seemed to be shaking his head in amused exasperation. What did that mean? That Fyfe didn't believe him? Fyfe knew about MacDuff. He knew why he had gone to Donaldson MacDuff. He knew what MacDuff's reaction had been. So why didn't he believe him then?

Ramensky let his head sink back. The thin mattress offered little cushioning from the hard surface of the platform beneath. He was, he realised with a tiny throat-scouring snort of frightened laughter, in the same cell he had woken up in earlier that day. The same graffiti was on the walls, and the same single light bulb hung from its flex on the ceiling. They had taken his trouser belt and his shoe laces again. He remembered walking out but after that everything was a complete blank until he came round and found himself back in the place he thought he had left. Suddenly, a sense of disorientation and imminent disaster crowded in on him as though the cell walls had tilted inwards. He rubbed his eyes and massaged his dry lips. He felt weak and unsteady even though he was lying on his back. His tongue was sore but the swelling seemed to have subsided and he was able to speak properly. He could taste a residue of sweet dark rum that coated the inside of his mouth.

'I didn't do it,' he repeated.

'We know exactly what you did,' Fyfe answered. 'We could have worked something out, Sandy. Why did you have to go and confess?'

Maybe Fyfe did know what he had done, Ramensky thought. Maybe he knew better than Ramensky himself. After all, he had no recollection of what had happened to him since leaving the police cell. Perhaps he had never left it, never got away from the land of the putty-faced people. It could be false, the memory of his belongings being poured out of the brown envelope, the point of the pen slowly scraping his name on the release form, the door opening on to the cold air of the outside world, and the friendly slap on his shoulder as he passed through. His inability to make himself understood could be a false memory too. It had all been a disjointed dream. MacDuff could be an imaginary character, another clown face conjured up on the spinning carousel. Perhaps he hadn't gone on a binge the previous night either, or perhaps he had and the death of Zena McElhose was an untrue invention of his short-circuiting brain.

Confusion caused Ramensky's throbbing headache to get worse. What was this confession Fyfe talked about? He sat up on the bunk, supporting himself in the corner, and moved his fingers up to his forehead and pressed hard to try and ease it. But it made no difference. There was no dispute that he was here in the police cell, so he must have done something to warrant being arrested. He had first met Fyfe when being questioned about old Zena's death, so she must be dead. And Fyfe knew about MacDuff, mentioning his name unprompted, so he had to be real too. Ramensky let his fingers slide up into his hair, gripping it and pulling. The ache inside his head rippled like a wave passing along a length of rope until the sudden sharp whip-crack at the end which made him grunt with pain as his whole body tensed and shuddered.

'I know what you've done, Sandy,' Fyfe was saying. 'I would have helped you. I would have seen you all right. Look at you now. You're a mess.'

Ramensky frowned. Keeping his eyes narrowed stopped his senses being flooded with too much light but it also made Fyfe a blurred, insubstantial figure. Ramensky didn't understand. What was Fyfe telling him? He knew how he had gone to Donaldson MacDuff to ask him to kill his employer, Zena McElhose, for a cash payment. MacDuff had refused and Ramensky couldn't get away quickly enough, although later he had considered going back to explain about his daughter Lorna and how he was only trying to save her by stealing old Zena's life force. Okay, it had been a crazy idea, but he was a grieving father wildly clutching at straws that he hoped would magically cure his dying daughter. Who could blame him?

155

'I understand, Sandy,' Fyfe said. 'I understand what you were trying to do. Believe me, I understand.'

It had been a crazy idea, Ramensky thought, yet maybe he had been crazy that night. He saw himself on his way home from work fighting off his attackers in the park, experienced again the mind-blasting rush of adrenalin that only gradually faded, like a tide going out. And he saw himself standing at his front door, looking up through the darkness towards the big house with its widely spaced security lights and thinking he saw furtive shapes dodge round the corner leading to the path to the rear. He thought there were two of them moving in single file but they were nothing more than a fleeting impression on the very fringe of his vision. And when he tried to look more closely, he noticed the big seagulls wheeling overhead that were sending shadows scuttling in different directions. He went inside and went to sleep. He didn't know what woke him in the morning, probably some kind of premonition because he had got out of bed much earlier than usual and was standing over Lorna's cot when he heard Marianne scream. Moments later he was standing over Zena McElhose's dead body and his first thought was that her death wouldn't help little Lorna at all. It was pointless. It had been a waste of time and effort for whoever had committed the crime.

'Why did you have to admit to it, Sandy? I would have helped you. You should have held out.'

Fyfe was on his feet. He went to the wash-hand basin, ran the tap. Water rattled noisily against the stainless steel making it vibrate. Ramensky wondered if, that night, he had indeed killed old Zena but then blacked it out in his own mind. Suppose he had followed the housebreaker inside, seen his chance to help Lorna and escape the blame by leaving a scapegoat behind, complete with murder weapon in his hand and incriminating balaclava. Ramensky tried to remember but it was all an impenetrable blank. He tried hard but the aching in his head screamed too painfully into a void and he couldn't handle it.

'Is that how you did it, Sandy?' Fyfe was asking, waving his hands in the air to dry them. 'Did you arrive back from work and see somebody up at the big house? Did you follow the bloke Randolph inside? Seize your chance in the hope of saving Lorna? Did you bludgeon Zena to death and then go for poor, unfortunate Randolph who got his kicks less bloodily just by breaking into houses? You definitely frightened him, Sandy. You must have thought your luck was in when he conveniently dropped down at your feet with a heart attack and you were able to put the mallet in his hand and go back to bed to wait for Marianne to discover the body.'

The sink gurgled loudly as the water ran away. Ramensky pulled his knees into the circle of his arms and trembled. It was uncanny how Fyfe read his thoughts and told him what he had done. He had been sleepwalking. He remembered writing his signature. He had thought it was a form to collect his belongings. It must have been a confession. He had thought he had seen Zena McElhose dead in the kitchen. He must have killed her in the kitchen the night before. Even if he couldn't remember it must be true.

'Why did you confess so easily, Sandy? I would have looked after you. At the very least I could have delayed things so that you could stay with Lorna. I would have done that for you. We could have worked something out. Pity. It's too late now.'

Ramensky shook his head. He watched Fyfe go over to the cell door. There was the sound of a key turning and it swung open. A pony's face with bared teeth leapt at him. A set of human teeth grinned. He flinched and held an arm in front of his face. A truncheon with the legend *A Present from Malaga* came flying towards him. He covered his head. The carousel above Lorna's cot spun into a blur. It went quiet then. Nothing else emerged to threaten him. Slowly he let his hands slide down his face until he could see through the spaces between his fingers and saw Fyfe standing in the doorway, shaking his head sadly.

'Too late now,' Fyfe said and then he was gone.

43

Monday, 16.05
There were more than thirty detectives in the incident room for Sir Duncan's big announcement. John Sapalski's desk had been emptied and tidied up. The time of his funeral was posted on

the noticeboard. Fyfe had discovered that nobody seemed to know what was going on. Even the turnkeys at St Leonards were unaware of any charges being made against Ramensky. They had no knowledge of him being questioned in connection with the McElhose murder. According to them, he had been lifted off the streets for fighting the night before, released in the morning, and brought back later, pissed out of his head once more. Somewhere in between he must have confessed to murder. Fyfe couldn't quite fit in the inter-connecting details but no doubt all would be explained when the Chief Constable told them how they should have been doing their jobs.

Fyfe waited in his own frosted-glass partition office until there was something for the crowd of standing and sitting bodies to focus on. He had tried to find Matthewson before the event but he was nowhere around. Now he appeared along with Graham Evans flanking Sir Duncan who was, for some reason, in his full dress uniform, polished silver buttons, peaked cap and all. Superintendent Les Cooper patted the air with his hands to quieten everybody down. The Chief Constable stood at the end of the room and waited for silence. Then he held up a plastic bag containing a white lump. Fyfe peered closely. From his distance he could not make out what it was, except that it was some kind of indistinct moulded shape.

'This', said Sir Duncan, his voice booming melodramatically, 'is a white soapstone parrot bookend.'

The roomful of detectives looked at each other surreptitiously during the pause that followed the statement. Nobody laughed, although a few raised their eyebrows. Others began to make connections. Fyfe frowned, thinking back to Ramensky staring at him in bewilderment from the corner of the yellow-walled police cell. Sir Duncan turned the plastic bag in towards his face to check its contents. Then he went on.

'It was one of several objects found in a cupboard at the home of Gregor Runciman, a senior partner in the law firm of Randolph and Runciman of which the late Valentine Randolph was also a senior partner. The parrot, this parrot, is one of a pair we know to be stolen. Its partner was found among a set of similar disparate objects in a cupboard in the home of Valentine Randolph when it was searched after he was discovered unconscious not far from the murder victim, Zena McElhose. Gregor Runciman has confessed to murdering Mrs McElhose.'

Fyfe's jaw dropped in astonishment. A trail of saliva had begun to run out of the corner of his mouth. He wiped it dry and kept his hand up at his face to hide his embarrassment. So Ramensky was innocent and the all-knowing performance of the wise detective in front of him an hour before had been totally unnecessary and wrong-headed. Fyfe had been absolutely convinced. An hour ago he would have bet his life savings, everything under the shed floor, on Ramensky's guilt and, from what he was being told, he would have lost the lot. Matthewson looked over at him and gave a barely discernible nod of confirmation. Hasn't Hunky Dunky done well, he silently implied.

'It seems that Val Randolph and Gregor Runciman spiced up their outwardly respectable lives by regularly going out at weekends to break into the houses of friends and acquaintances. It was, apparently, the revival of a game they played while studying law together at university and which had fallen into abeyance before the death of Randolph's wife started it up again. They had a strict policy of targeting people they knew socially or in a business sense and of breaking into houses they had already visited, often stealing and copying keys so that entry would be relatively simple. They also took inconsequential items that the owners would hardly notice were missing and, even if they did, would never bother reporting to the police. I know, both Randolph and Gregor Runciman have been dinner guests at my home. The parrot bookends are my property. Funny, isn't it, what some people will do for weekend entertainment?'

There was a ripple of restrained laughter at Sir Duncan's little joke. Fyfe laughed louder than most. Runciman had been with the Chief Constable in the canteen the day before, so blended into the background that Fyfe couldn't put a face to the name. He would have eventually got round to questioning him, he supposed, but had never contemplated the possibility of Runciman's involvement in old Zena's murder. Perhaps he just hadn't had time. Now a photograph of Runciman was being passed round. It was a happy snap of some kind of office night out. Runciman and Randolph, red-eyed in the blast of flash, were wearing conical party hats and holding colourful drinks with straws and cocktail umbrellas stick-

159

ing up out of them. Runciman was a stooping hatchet-faced man with sinister bundles of laugh-lines at the corner of his eyes. He looked faintly ridiculous and completely harmless, the kind of respectable establishment type you would expect to find at a Chief Constable's dinner party. How wrong can you get?

Fyfe handed on the photograph. He should have been checking on all Randolph's close friends and business contacts. But he hadn't bothered. Instead, he had gone to lunch with Angela while singling out Ramensky for the full treatment and uncovering enough circumstantial evidence to have him hung from the nearest lamppost. Only Fyfe had just about intended to take it upon himself to conceal Ramensky's guilt on the grounds that the balance of his mind had been disturbed by the fact that his daughter had a terminal illness. His role as protector, however, had proved illusory. He had actually been a false accuser, acting with the righteous zeal of a Witchfinder General even if it was with the best of intentions. There was a real paradox. Fyfe couldn't help laughing out loud.

'They worked as a team,' Sir Duncan explained, squirting the words out from behind a hugely self-satisfied grin. 'The overalls and balaclavas were part of the ritual. According to Runciman, he was trying to wind the whole thing up and Randolph had agreed to stop once they had worked their way through the church congregation where they were both members. Then they picked Zena McElhose as a victim, stole her keys at a coffee morning in the church hall, and broke in on Saturday night. She had told them she was going away for the weekend but she must have changed her mind because she disturbed them in the kitchen. Runciman panicked, grabbed the first weapon that came to hand, the meat tenderiser, and lashed out. The shock and stress of the situation caused Randolph to go into cardiac arrest. He collapsed and Runciman didn't have the strength to get him out of the house, so he left him there to take all the blame. Runciman thought Randolph was dead and it was only once the bodies were found that he realised he was still alive and almost certain to implicate him when he regained consciousness, so he came to me, as he had come to dinner in my house, to confess this morning. When he did so he was not aware that Randolph had died in hospital and he was, effectively, in the clear, ironic or what?'

Fyfe nodded in mute agreement. Irony was the pervasive

background colour to this episode. It meant that Sandy Ramensky's homicidal fantasies were always just that despite Fyfe's assumption that there was no smoke without fire. It meant that Maureen Gilliland, the suicide driver in the blood red Mercedes, had invented her love affair with Randolph on the spur of the moment to create a fantasy life for herself that others might envy as she died in a blaze of passionate glory. Sapalski's death was an unfortunate consequence of a head-on collision between fantasy and reality. Fyfe had been a victim of that kind of collision as well, but all that had happened to him was a rather pleasant lunch in a posh hotel and some lipstick on his cheek as a going-away present.

Sir Duncan rambled on. He stuffed his pipe with tobacco but didn't light it because the incident room was designated 'No Smoking'. He answered questions from the floor, enjoyed being in the spotlight and being seen to be leading from the front by bringing in his own prisoners. The confession was signed. Charges had been laid and the report would be with the fiscal within the next few hours. He tidied away all the irritating loose ends and tied a lovely bow round the whole investigation. Eventually, with responsibility for the paperwork delegated, the session broke up and the gaggle of detectives settled back to the more mundane tasks allocated to them by a disintegrating society. Sir Duncan came over to Fyfe.

'I hear that McElhose's handyman chap Ramensky is in custody.'

'That's right,' Fyfe answered.

'He has a sickly child, I believe.'

'Poor bastard went on a drinking binge. He was terrified we were going to pin Zena's murder on him. I tried to persuade him otherwise but he wouldn't listen. He's banged up for conduct liable.'

Sir Duncan sighed. 'Irrational, but I suppose with his family circumstances entirely understandable. A degree of mercy is in order. Can you see to it he's all right?'

Fyfe had to swallow hard to be able to speak. 'I can manage that.'

'Reassure him. Take him home.'

'No problem, sir.' He rubbed the back of his neck. 'I'll see to it straight away.'

161

44

Ramensky was enveloped in a hug from Marianne as soon as he entered the living-room. She had Lorna balanced by her left arm on one hip and she threw her other arm round his neck, standing on her toes and pressing her face into the side of his neck. Neither said anything. Lorna surveyed the scene solemnly through her large eyes like a third, partially formed head that had grown on the edge of the strange biological beast that was made up by the entwined bodies of her two parents. She was part of them, yet somehow detached. Her deathly pale skin was translucent, her thin hair so fine compared to their rude health. She had her own independent existence, albeit one that was withering away fast in front of Fyfe's eyes. It was a pity Ramensky's crazy theory of stealing life from other people to save the little girl didn't seem to work. Old Zena was dead and it looked as if young Lorna would shortly follow her, so it was just as well that he hadn't turned murderer. At least, Ramensky would not be behind bars when the time came. He could watch her die and suffer the grief and loss at first hand. Fyfe would have guaranteed him that fate even if Ramensky had killed Zena. Fyfe wouldn't have cared if nobody thanked him.

He had collected his dented Volvo from the mechanics and driven away while the celebration party was still under way at headquarters. Big Chief Constable, ignoring the no-smoking rule, was leading his detective braves in a triumphal dance round the force's totem pole. Good luck to him, Fyfe thought grudgingly. He deserved the credit. Fyfe was just pleased that his magnanimous attempt to protect Ramensky from the law had included a selfish aversion to sharing his carefully constructed alternative solution to the murder mystery with anyone else.

'Would you like a cup of tea, Mr Fyfe?' Marianne asked.

'No. No thank you. I really must be going.'

Ramensky and Marianne had drawn apart. He knew they didn't want him there. They wanted to be alone with their child.

That was what he wanted for them too. But politeness dictated that he had to be offered hospitality, and the rituals, like short courses of drug treatments, had to be observed. This time, though, he wasn't going to make the mistake of asking how Lorna was. He tried to make stupid mistakes like that only once: Life was a long, drawn-out learning process. He held out a hand to the girl and she clutched his index finger. There seemed to be hardly any strength in her grip. When he pulled his finger away there was no resistance.

'Are you sure?'

'Absolutely certain. I'm still on duty.'

'Something a little stronger?'

'No. Honestly.'

'Thank you anyway for bringing him home to me.'

'Don't mention it. Don't be too hard on him.'

'I'll try not to be.'

'Just keep him out of trouble.'

'I will.'

She smiled benignly, a powerful matriarchal figure accepting the aberrant male back into her home. Fyfe didn't know if she was aware of Ramensky's abortive attempt to hire a contract killer on behalf of little Lorna. He had a feeling that maybe she was the real decision-maker in the household who had told him not to be so stupid when he outlined the extent of his dabbling in the dubious pseudo-science of metempsychosis. She must have been worried that he had ignored her when she found Zena's body in the kitchen at the end of the driveway, more so when he vanished on a drinking binge. But it had all come good. Fyfe had given a rudimentary explanation of Runciman's unexpected confession over the phone. Now Marianne and Ramensky could return to what passed for normal for them. They could turn their backs on the world, hold hands and wait for Lorna to die.

Ramensky took his child and sat in the armchair with her held close in against his chest. Fyfe had pulled rank to retrieve him from the holding cells in plenty of time to prevent the fiscal becoming involved. Ramensky was as withdrawn and uncooperative as he had been during Fyfe's previous visit until he began to appreciate that he had been exonerated by events elsewhere. At first, he seemed to think Fyfe was springing him despite an overwhelming prosecution case. It was only then Fyfe realised that Ramensky himself was not totally convinced of his own innocence. He laced his shoes and snatched up his poured-out belongings for the second time that day with a haste that underlined his eagerness to take advantage of the situation before somebody somewhere changed his mind again.

'You mean I didn't do it?' he asked earnestly in the car.

'So you kept telling me, didn't you?' Fyfe replied.

'But you said you knew I had done it.'

'Not quite. Not quite.'

Fyfe skirted round the awkward fact that he had until approximately one hour before firmly believed that Ramensky was guilty. Fortunately, he had tried to convey his message to Ramensky in coded language so that they could keep it secret between themselves. He had even, thinking he was being incredibly clever, indulged in a pantomime display of washing his hands to suggest absolution. If it hadn't gone over Ramensky's head it had obviously gone shooting off at a tangent. That, and Ramensky being pretty pissed at the time, allowed Fyfe to reasonably pretend a misunderstanding had occurred and Fyfe didn't have to admit publicly to being a complete fool.

'What I meant was I knew how far you had gone, but I also knew you hadn't gone the final step to cold-blooded murder. Nobody else needs to know. Especially now.'

'Oh.'

'So, you see, Sandy, everything's worked out for the best in the end.'

'Yes. It has, hasn't it?'

And there Ramensky was, safely delivered as Fyfe had promised to the armchair by the fireside with his child on his lap and his devoted wife kneeling in front of him. It was a still-life cameo of perfect domestic bliss, spoiled only by Lorna's big eyes, their luminosity flickering uncertainly like wind-disturbed candle flames, staring after Fyfe as he closed the door. A suffocating sense of sadness draped itself round him. He leaned against the wall until the terrible tightness had passed and he was able to breathe easily.

Outside on the doorstep, Fyfe looked up at the darkening sky and felt the wetness of the tiny drops burst over the skin of his face. He opened his mouth to drink the miniature capsules of

164

stinging rain. He thought of Zena McElhose, and Maureen Gilliland, and John Sapalski, and little Lorna's approaching death, and his own. Where do human souls go when the bodies die, he wondered?

45

Monday, 17.56

Fyfe parked his car on the opposite side of the street to Hilary's flat and settled down to watch. The lights were on and the curtains open. He could see the top of the table lamp and the mirror above the sofa where they had lain together. Once he thought he caught a glimpse of somebody moving on the edge of the framed scene, momentarily breaking its symmetry like ripples radiating out from a small stone thrown into calm water that quickly settles again. He remembered seeing his own reflection in the mirror, arm round Hilary, the rest of the room distorted by the bevelled edge as though they had been dropped into an exact centre, creating the disturbance. It had been scary.

From the car Fyfe stared upwards, not really concentrating. There were thousands of other rooms in the city, millions all over the country, where strange things were going on, inexplicable to anyone not involved or associated with them and sometimes impossible to understand even then. Feelings of depression made the pale darkness outside grow blacker. Fyfe scratched his head and cupped the back of his neck in a supporting hand. Lives were played out in a wilderness of broken mirrors, a fractured world of coincidence and cross purpose that produced the interlinking chains of circumstance that eventually resulted in death and tragedy, or less intimidating outcomes such as him sitting outside the home of a prospective lover. But that wasn't the end of it surely? The chain might, almost certainly would, run on. What next? Which way would new reflections bounce? What would the final picture show?

The heater was running, pouring warm air round him. He stretched one leg out over the passenger seat to make himself comfortable. He willed Hilary to phone him and waited patiently as the car's air-conditioning system fought a losing battle against his breathing and all around him the glass steamed up. Warmth and weariness made his eyes heavy and his brain slow. The sharp edges of Hilary's clearly defined first-floor location blurred. When the phone rang he jerked in surprise and hit his knee on the dashboard in his haste to answer it.

'Bill Matthewson here.'

'Good to hear from you, Bill.' Fyfe excised the disappointment from his voice. 'Missing me already, are you?'

'John's wife Wilma went into premature labour. She was rushed to hospital.'

Fyfe had to think before he knew who John and Wilma were. It produced the contrast of Sapalski's crushed and flattened body laid out on the lawn and his wife Wilma's hugely pregnant form upright in the chair. It should not have been funny and Fyfe was ashamed of himself when he was unable to suppress a sardonic smile.

'I thought you would appreciate knowing,' Matthewson was saying. 'She's had the baby. By all accounts it's fine. Small but perfectly formed. We've had a whip round for a bunch of flowers and a card. I put in a couple of quid for you.'

'Thanks. I'll pay you back.'

'It's just good to be able to pass on some good news for a change.'

'I know what you mean.'

Matthewson hung up. Through wet opaqueness on the glass, Fyfe noticed movement at Hilary's window. He scrambled to drag his leg back and be able to reach over to wipe a hole in the condensation. By then the curtains were closed, shutting him off. He punched Hilary's number into the handset and watched the window as the ringing echoed in his ear.

'Hi,' he said when he heard her voice. 'This is a voice from your recent past.'

'So it is. How are you?'

Fyfe had an image of Hilary's lips shaping the words. 'I'm fine. Can you talk?'

'Yes, of course. Are you on or off duty?'

'Off. Case closed. The fabric of society has been stitched back together.'

'That's good to know. Where are you?'

'Not far away. I was wondering if I might make you an offer?'

'Do you think that is wise?'

'Probably not. You could be a dangerous woman to know.'

'How dangerous?'

'Very dangerous.'

'But you're still going to ask me?'

'I'm afraid so.'

'Go on then.' Hilary laughed and the sound seemed to provoke a sudden flurry of snow that obscured her window and enveloped the entire street in a white-out. 'Don't be afraid. I can only say no.'

46

Monday, 18.30

What was he doing here? Fyfe wasn't exactly sure. It had been a spur of the moment decision to come to the hospital, buy a bunch of red carnations at the shop, and go looking for Wilma Sapalski in the maternity wing that smelled of disinfectant and cleanliness. He had time to spare, provided he didn't take too long. It was only about an hour's drive north over the Forth Bridge and on to Gleneagles so that he could organise the hotel room in advance of his promised visitor. He had plenty of time.

Wilma was at the end of a labyrinth of long green corridors that dwindled to a converging point in the distance like railway lines. She was sound asleep and Fyfe was grateful because now that he was there he had no idea what he would have said to her. The ward sister was a plump middle-aged woman with a kindly face and a smoker's deep-throated voice. She asked him if he was the husband and nodded sagely when he said he was just a friend. She showed him to the bed with a finger pressed to her lips. She took the flowers, said she would put them in water and cradled them, probably from force of habit, as if they were a new-born baby.

'Would you like to see the baby?' she asked. 'He's in the

special care nursery. He's a bit early, you see. Under three pounds. He didn't wait for a formal invitation. Oh well, boys will be boys.'

Fyfe followed her towards the lights at the end of another long corridor. There, a room was full of incubators with tiny scraps of babies in them, arms and legs punching the air as though they were wrestling with invisible enemies in the desperate fight to stay alive. Nurses moved among the plastic boxes responding to a series of cries and whimpers. Wilma's baby was barely the size of Fyfe's hand, its limbs thinner than his fingers, its skin all wrinkled and red. It had wires taped to it and a tube up its nose. Its legs were curled up to its stomach where the cut cord still protruded and was held by some kind of clamp. Its head, covered in an old-fashioned woollen bonnet, seemed disproportionately large. Its eyes were puffy and tightly closed, its eyelids pink and almost transparent. The expression on its face changed with every flex and twitch of its arms as though it was mentally concentrating on silent music that dictated a private dance.

'Does he have a name?' Fyfe asked.

'Not yet,' the nurse replied in a hoarse whisper.

Fyfe looked down on the baby and thought how, at the moment, it would have been more at home in the womb than in the real world. Yet it would not be long before it developed and grew strong, ready for the transformation from baby to child to adult in a few short, accelerating years. All weekend he had been dealing with death and dying. Now he was witnessing the beginning of a pristine new life with a future that was impossible to know stretching ahead like an endless corridor. He wondered where its soul had come from, where its soul had been. It made the skin of his face sting as if it was being pricked all over by a thousand needle-sharp points.

'Good luck to you, kid,' he muttered quietly before turning and walking away.

47

David Fyfe had to lean all the way across the wide bed to grope
for the softly burring phone. Not yet properly awake, he mis-
judged the distance and fell on his face. His clumsy fingers
pushed the receiver off the table and it vanished down the side
of the bed. He gritted his teeth, bracing himself for the clatter
when it hit the floor. When none came his fuzzy brain could not
understand. He crawled the extra six inches over the bed to look
down over the side. There he saw the main part of the phone
lying, almost floating, on a blue carpet with a lavishly deep pile.
The bone-shaped receiver was floating too, connected by its
spiral cord. A tiny voice was speaking from it, a distant whisper,
thin as a wisp of smoke. He scooped it up and held it to his ear.

'Your wife is on her way up, Mr Fyfe,' it said.

'But I'm not married,' he blurted out.

A delightfully feminine peal of laughter, reminiscent of giggling teenage girls on a sunlit hillside, ended the brief exchange
that reminded him where he was and what he had done. Hilary,
unseen just like the downstairs receptionist, had been the last
woman to laugh like that when he had propositioned her.

It all came back in a rush as he rolled off the bed and
reassembled the phone before putting it back on the bedside
table. He was at the Gleneagles Hotel, making quick use of his
golf outing raffle prize of a free night. When he arrived through
the blizzard in his battered Volvo the staff couldn't do enough
for him. He had been gratuitously upgraded from standard
double room to luxury suite with bedroom and sitting-room.
There was a complimentary bottle of good champagne in an ice
bucket, an overflowing fruit basket, and a bathroom stuffed with
sweet-smelling toiletries. He was told a full meal would be
served in the room whenever he wanted it. He had showered,
shaved, and wrapped himself up in the fluffiest dressing-gown
he had ever seen. He had got carried away and unwisely raided
the mini-bar. He had mixed himself a large whisky and bitter

lemon, toasted John Sapalski's new-born son and Sandy Ramensky's dying daughter, and almost immediately crashed out on the king-size bed.

Fyfe helped himself to another whisky and emptied the bitter lemon bottle into it. He sat in a chair facing the door to the lobby and waited for his wife to join him. He worked out that it had been less than forty-eight hours, a mere two days, since his first encounter with Hilary yet it already seemed like an episode from ancient history. He seemed to have known her and been kissing friends with her all his life. The pace of events since she materialised in front of him at the Saturday night party had been fast and ferocious. He had hardly slept since then, always conscious that while he was drinking in the sight of Hilary in her clinging black dress, Angela was looking up his number in her address book, Zena McElhose's skull was being cracked open with the meat mallet, Valentine Randolph's heart was beginning to beat irregularly, and guilt was getting a grip on Gregor Runciman. The following chain of unpredictable consequence claimed the lives of Maureen Gilliland and John Sapalski, but for some inscrutable reason didn't permit Sandy Ramensky to throw himself to his death off the parapet of a high bridge. Fyfe in his professional analysis of the situation got the workings utterly and totally wrong but thankfully nobody need ever know that he was the world's worst detective. Didn't time pass quickly when you were enjoying yourself?

He sipped his whisky and smiled. Now he could afford to sit back and draw breath. Maybe he should attribute his failings to lack of sleep, he thought, or maybe lack of wakefulness. He had dreamed it all and then woken up to a different reality. Wait a minute though, he was still sleepy. Perhaps he was still dreaming. Never mind, there would be other weekends.

Fyfe crossed his legs and arranged the dressing-gown decorously over them. He examined the embroidered monogram on the breast pocket and brushed some stray flecks from it. She should have reached the room by now. He estimated it should take two minutes, no more, by either stair or lift. He stared at the wall and imagined her coming along the corridor, her footsteps muffled by the thick carpet. The knock on the door was right on cue. He jumped up to answer it. Sally stood beaming on the other side. There was snow on her shoulders and in her hair.

She stepped forward, kicked off her shoes, and kissed him on the lips in intimate greeting.

'So you do have romance in your soul,' she said.

'Did you ever doubt it?'

'Of course not, darling. But at such short notice.'

'Come into my parlour.' He waved a hand at the interior. 'Welcome to the combat zone. Monday nights may never be the same again.'

'This is great.' She handed him an overnight bag with the change of clothes he had asked for. 'I'm really glad you invited me.'

'Well, my other lover couldn't make it.'

'No. I mean it.' She kissed him again before walking past to begin a detailed inspection of the suite. 'I'm really glad.'

'So am I.'

Fyfe closed the door. There was no point in spoiling what was left of the evening by telling Sally that she was there because Hilary had turned him down, probably not quite believing he was serious. The drunken philosopher at the Saturday night party had not revealed the logic-busting solution to old Zeno's paradox so Fyfe had not yet managed to cover the distance between him and Hilary. Maybe he had got half-way, but they remained as far apart as ever.

Sally knew him better, however. He and Sally had been travelling together for a long time. He reached out and stroked her arm as she passed. They had been through a lot. There was no longer any distance between them that any philosopher would ever be able to measure. She did not have to be asked twice when he asked her to drop everything and come to Gleneagles. She dumped the dogs with her cousin Catriona on the way north but he kept thinking he saw them running about the room. They were a team, him and Sally and the dogs. He watched her move round the room touching things here and there to check they were real. He loved her, didn't he? Yes, he did. Then why ruin a beautiful relationship by letting the truth intrude? He went to the ice bucket and began to unwrap the foil from the cork on the champagne.

'Sally.'

'What?' She turned in the bedroom doorway, looking back questioningly, leaving her body facing the other way.

'Will you marry me?'

'What? Again?'

'Sure. Why not?'

'Let's talk about it in the morning.'

He didn't want to spoil the mood so he didn't argue. She went into the bedroom and dived head first on to the bed. The cork popped. The champagne foamed and Fyfe caught most of it in a tall flute glass. Sally came hurrying back and grabbed the other one of the pair. The contact of bottle neck on glass rim made a clear ringing noise. Sally laughed. All good things come in threes, Fyfe thought. He waited until the champagne bubbles settled and then drank a mouthful. It tickled the back of his throat and his nose. The alcohol hit him like a slap on the back from an old friend, slackening his hold on reality. He was tired and drunk but at least he was safe. The snow was falling silently outside, whirling through the air, spinning a temporary cocoon where they could curl up in perfect safety.

'Cheers,' said Sally.

'Likewise,' Fyfe said.

'You certainly know how to treat a woman.'

'I have a masters degree in it.'

'And you're still learning.'

'Here's to the future.'

Sally put her arms round him and hugged him close. Fyfe rested his chin on her shoulder and filled his glass behind her back. He could feel her soft breasts pressed against his chest and the firm beating of her heart. He could taste the bubbles fizzing on his tongue. He closed his eyes and enjoyed the dream.